"After working here, and then at the diner, you get to do homework duty at night?" Matt asked.

Callie glanced up and nodded, as if perplexed. "Of course."

He'd have given anything to have a mother like that, a mother who was invested in her kid. He'd tackled his difficulties in school on his own and failed miserably. "That's amazing, Callie."

She glanced up. Their gazes met.

She went still, her eyes on his.

And she read his gaze, his thoughts. It was there in her slight intake of breath, the way she blinked, the quick flex of fingers as if realization just struck.

"I've got to reload the nail guns," she said, breaking the connection. But that was good, right? Neither one of them had the time or energy to put into whatever was flaring between them, so it was best to ignore it.

But there was no way in this world he'd be able to ignore Callie for the coming weeks, and a big part of him didn't want to try.

And that spelled trouble for both of them.

Books by Ruth Logan Herne

Love Inspired

Winter's End
Waiting Out the Storm
Made to Order Family
*Reunited Hearts
*Small-Town Hearts
*Mended Hearts
*Yuletide Hearts

*Men of Allegany County

RUTH LOGAN HERNE

Born into poverty, Ruth puts great stock in one of her favorite Ben Franklinisms: "Having been poor is no shame. Being ashamed of it is." With God-given appreciation for the amazing opportunities abounding in our land, Ruth finds simple gifts in the everyday blessings of smudge-faced small children, bright flowers, fresh baked goods, good friends, family, puppies and higher education. She believes a good woman should never fear dirt, snakes or spiders, all of which like to infest her aged farmhouse, necessitating a good pair of tongs for extracting the snakes, a flat-bottomed shoe for the spiders, and the dirt…

Simply put, she's learned that some things aren't worth fretting about! If you laugh in the face of dust and love to talk about God, men, romance, great shoes and wonderful food, feel free to contact Ruth through her website at www.ruthloganherne.com.

Yuletide Hearts

Ruth Logan Herne

Love Inspired

Recycling programs for this product may not exist in your area.

 LOVE INSPIRED BOOKS

ISBN-13: 978-0-373-81592-0

YULETIDE HEARTS

www.LoveInspiredBooks.com

Printed in U.S.A.

My son, if your heart is wise, then my heart will be glad; my inmost being will rejoice when your lips speak what is right.
—*Proverbs* 23:15–16

This book is dedicated to my mother-in-law, Theresa Elizabeth Blodgett, a woman who has never been afraid to put her hand to any task, large or small. Her strength and devotion are a constant inspiration to me. She's one of those gals who could have settled the west single-handedly and would have coffee waiting for the crew at day's end. Merry Christmas, Mom!

Acknowledgments

Big thanks to Bob Dean of Dean Remodeling in Hilton, New York, known affectionately as "Bob the Builder." Bob's advice on construction and his dedication to a job well done helped lay the foundation for Cobbled Creek. Huge thanks to Karen and Don Ash of the Angelica Sweet Shop and The Black-Eyed Susan Café in Angelica, New York, for getting behind this project. You guys are truly amazing! Hugs and gratitude to Major Tony Giusti and his lovely wife Debby (my Seekerville sister) for their sage advice on military basics. I'm spoiled to call so many experts "friends."

To Beth for finding silly mistakes… And there were several! To Mandy for being my right-hand gal on road trips and for giving me a namesake. I love both! To Jon, who has taken on stove and refrigerator duty. You rock! To Stacey and Lisa for the spontaneous gifts of coffee: You have no idea how that spurs me to work into the night. Thank you! Hugs and thanks to Kyle and Casey Kenyon. I don't know what I'd do without you guys. And always to Dave, whose work ethic inspires my own: Thanks for the sandwiches. And the coffee, Dude. And for being there, night and day.

Chapter One

Complete and utter desolation.

Peering through a driving November downpour caused by remnants of Hurricane Karl, Matt Cavanaugh surveyed what might be the biggest mistake he ever made as sheeting water sluiced from unprotected roofs. Wind-driven storm rains pummeled gaping window openings. Expensive, irreplaceable topsoil washed down unprotected berms, each muddy water trail sweeping centuries of rich, organic soil into the watershed.

Basically he was watching a large share of his life savings wash away. What had he been thinking?

"I see merit here, son."

The memory of his grandfather's reassuring voice eased the tension snaking Matt's back, crowding his neck. Simple words from a gentle man, an industrious construction worker unafraid to lift a hand to any task, great or small, including the gift of unconditional love to his bad-boy grandson.

Matt clenched his jaw, then realized that would only fuel headache potential. Surveying the muddy mess he'd just purchased with significant help from the bank, he fought the urge to run hard, fast and long when a banging screen door drew his attention to the left.

A boy raced out of the faded farmhouse facing the neglected subdivision. A dog chased after him, a black-and-white spitfire, his non-pedigreed look perfect for the place and the boy, a pair of mutts enjoying the tempest.

Within seconds they were soaked, the rain blurring their features, but the combined excitement apparent even from this distance.

The boy aimed for the uncompleted subdivision, the dog racing alongside. Too late, Matt realized their intent.

The kid dived through a window opening.

The dog followed.

The kid emerged from a door opening.

So did the mutt.

Then back in another window, a little higher this time, the crazy game of follow the leader probably not the smartest of ideas for a kid and a dog around a construction site. Matt left his truck at the now-unnecessary roadblock and raced downhill. "Hey! Hey, you! Kid. Stop."

Visions of leftover two-by-fours, nails, screws and abandoned tools raced through his head, the innocence of youth unfettered by the hazards of life. As the new owner, Matt didn't have the luxury of relaxation. Construction insurance rates skyrocketed with a claim, and the kid and the dog were a hospital visit waiting to happen. "Kid. Stop! Now!"

The driving rain swallowed his voice and the thickening mud did a similar number on his feet. The dress shoes he put on for the bank closing weren't meant for tromping around construction sites.

He lost visual of the quick-paced pair as he neared the skeletal houses, his descent and the rising rooflines blocking his line of sight. He wasn't sure if the storm made it impossible to hear the kid and the dog or if they were just unusually quiet. Since unusually quiet might mean unconscious, Matt increased his pace. "Kid! You hear me? Come out of there!"

No answer.

Matt continued along the road, mud-slicked shoes slowing his progress. The graveled areas would have been inconsequential in his boots. In worn dress shoes, the rough curves and sharp points of stone reminded him that if new shoes hadn't been on the list before, they'd gain a spot now, and all because some fool didn't have sense enough to keep their kid out of harm's way.

Kind of like his mother.

He refused to flinch at the memory. His mother was no June Cleaver, but he hadn't been a choirboy either. He had the juvie record to prove his stupidity before Grandpa Gus realigned him with old-fashioned hard work, faith and fishing.

A movement drew his attention left. He darted between two incomplete houses, saw the kid about a house-and-a-half away, yelled again and took off in pursuit. The boy appeared fairly savvy about dodging among the half-built homes, so Matt ducked through a window and raced across the subflooring to the front door of the house, burst through and collared the kid just as he angled toward the house Matt had cut through.

"Hey! Hey! Let go! Let me go!"

"Not until we've had a few words, kid."

"Let me go! Let me go!"

Matt held tight.

The dog raced into the fray, tail wagging, obviously unconcerned about his young owner's welfare.

"Jake? Jake? Where are you?"

The dog's tail flagged faster. He dashed to the front door of the house, barked a welcome, then raced back, his gaze expectant, his angled doggie look wondering what was going on.

Which reflected Matt's feelings to a tee.

A disheveled woman strode through the nonexistent front door, her hair a mess, her shoes not quite as bad as Matt's, her jeans rain-spattered, her fleece pullover soaked.

"In here, Mom! Someone's got me!"

"Someone's got you all right." Matt sent the kid a look meant to quell and refused to relinquish his grasp, despite the fire-breathing mother striding his way. Her purposeful gait seemed militaristic even though she wore somewhat impressive heeled boots, which meant she'd most likely served at some point in time. If that assumption proved true, she should know enough to keep her kid where he belonged.

He raised his chin, noted she almost matched him in height with the shoes on, met her glare and stood his ground, refusing to scowl, letting his stance make his point. "This your kid?"

"Let him go."

Matt ignored the command. "Do you have any idea how dangerous it is to have a kid running around a construction site? The things that could happen to him?"

The woman's gaze returned his look, one on one. "I'm well aware, thank you very much, although Jake knows his way around construction sites. Usually." She leveled a tough, knowing look to the kid, shoulders back, feet braced, her posture adding evidence to Matt's guess that she'd been in the military at one time. "Were you supposed to leave the house?"

"N-no."

"And what if something happened to The General?"

The General? Matt frowned, followed her glance to the dog and realized it must be the dog's name.

The boy snorted, a pretty gutsy act for a kid being collared by an absolute stranger while his mother reamed him out from a few feet away. "The General knows all the enemy hideouts. He's trained to sniff out snipers and UXBs."

"UXBs?"

The woman kept her gaze on the boy, her profile taut, worry lines marring a perfect forehead over sea-green eyes. Light brown hair fell to her shoulders, a side clip meant to keep the bulk of it out of her face, but the storm had outmaneuvered the clip's potential. She shoved the errant hair back, obviously irked. "Unexploded bombs. London. The Luftwaffe."

"I get the war reference." Matt switched his gaze from her to the kid as he released the boy's collar. "What I don't get is how *he* gets it. You're what? Seven? Eight?"

"Almost nine."

"Which means eight."

The kid's glare matched his mother's, obviously a genetic trait. "You can't play around these houses. It's off limits," Matt told him, his voice stern. He turned his attention to the woman, realizing she was probably chilled through, the November day wretchedly wet and cool. "You'll keep him out of here?"

"Yes." Something in her look told Matt she didn't say things lightly. That quality reassured him. She turned and hooked her thumb toward the door. "Jake, let's go. The banker's got better things to do than chase you around where you don't belong."

Her words registered as she neared the door, the kid following, head down, chin thrust out, forehead furrowed. "I'm not a banker." Matt strode forward and yanked down a bill of foreclosure notice attached to the front window. "I'm the new owner."

Her head jerked up. She stared at him, then the house, then him again, utter disappointment painting her features. Wet, bedraggled, rumpled, cold and wickedly disappointed.

Her look grabbed a piece of him, the air of disillusionment needing comfort and joy, but at the moment, confronted with the enormity of what he'd undertaken less than two hours ago, Matt's personal comfort level had nose-dived into incredulity.

"Seek and ye shall find. Knock, and the door will be opened, son."

Gus's wisdom reminded Matt that he wasn't in this alone, that despite Gus's death while Matt served in the desert sands of Iraq, he'd never be alone again, not in spirit anyway.

"You bought this house?"

The reality of the recent transaction tightened his neck, his look. "I bought the subdivision."

"All of it?" The kid's air reflected his mother's again, a shadowed starkness making Matt feel like a crusty headmaster, cold, cruel and crotchety.

The cold part was accurate, his wet clothes and the brisk wind a chilling reminder of what was to come. He met the kid's eyes and nodded. "All of it. Yes."

"But, Mom—"

"Stop, Jake. It's all right."

"But—"

"I said stop."

The kid's baffled look made Matt feel like scum, but why? Why should it matter if…

"You bought Cobbled Creek?"

A new voice entered the fray.

Matt swung around.

Three older men stood at the back door opening, backs straight, heads up, their posture definitely not at ease.

Military men, despite the paunch of one and the silver hair of another.

The man in the middle stepped forward, drew a breath and extended a hand. "I'm Hank Marek."

The name sent a warning bell of empathy. Hank Marek of Marek Home Builders, the now-defunct contractor that started this project over two years ago.

Matt wasn't a sympathetic person by nature. He'd hard-scrabbled his way up the ladder of success despite illegitimate beginnings followed by a fairly miserable upbringing, but coming face to face with the man who lost his dream so that Matt could have his, well…

He hauled in a breath and accepted Hank's hand. "Matt Cavanaugh of Cavanaugh Construction."

The older man's face revealed nothing of what he must be feeling inside, the loss of his work, his livelihood, his well-designed subdivision the victim of overextended loans and the burst of the housing bubble.

The other men stepped forward, concerned.

Hank moved back, nodded and directed a look beyond Matt to the woman and boy. "There's stew just about ready and the temperature's supposed to dip lower tonight before coming back up tomorrow. Jake, can you help me fire up the wood stove?"

The boy scowled Matt's way, scuffed a toe, huffed a sigh, then trudged past Matt, the dog trailing behind, their mutual postures voicing silent displeasure.

"Callie? I'll see you at home?"

"I'm on my way, Dad." She pivoted, her mud-slicked heel tipping the move.

Matt started to lean forward to stop her fall, but she managed to right herself despite the wet floor and the mud. High, flat, wedged heels marked her departure with a tap, tap, tap as she hung a right turn at the door. She strode up the drive to her car, the soaking rain deepening the pathos of an already melodramatic situation.

Matt watched her go, then headed to the back door opening. The older men and the boy trudged in measured steps across the banked field, faded flag stakes symbolizing the wear and tear of waiting through too many seasons of sun, wind, snow and rain.

Matt watched their progress, his brain working overtime, the reality hitting him.

Hank Marek lived alongside the subdivision he had tried to create in the beautiful hillside setting, the curving road nestling the homes in the ascending crook of the Allegheny foothills.

It was that eye for setting that drew Matt to the initial showing, then the ensuing auction, his appreciation for the timeless, reasonably priced and aesthetically pleasing housing, a plan that not only fit the terrain but added to it, a rarity.

But he had no idea Hank lived in the quaint, small farmhouse on the main road, just steps away from the sign labeling Cobbled Creek a community of fine, affordable homes.

He pinched the bridge of his nose, muttered a prayer that combined a plea for understanding and a silent lament that he might be following the foolish imprint of the older man's footsteps, and headed to his truck, the cold, soaking rain a reminder that winter loomed, and he had an amazing amount of work to do in a very limited time frame.

Which was probably something he should have thought a little more about before papers were signed and money exchanged, but the delayed closing was the bank's fault, not his. Matt understood the time constraints he faced, but God had guided him this far. Someway, somehow, they'd get these sweet homes battened down for the winter.

As he crested the rise to his truck, the woman's car backed toward the roadway, a wise decision on her part. Mud-slicked shoulders weren't to be trusted in these conditions, and when she curved the car expertly onto the road, then proceeded to the farmhouse beyond, he recognized the meaning behind Hank Marek's words.

The woman and the kid probably hated him for who he was and what he'd done. On top of that, they appeared to live across the street from where he would take over Hank's dream because he was lucky enough to be in the right place at the right time.

The hinted headache surged into full-blown reality, a niggling condition spawned from a really nasty concussion while fighting in Iraq, a grenade explosion too close for comfort. But if occasional bad headaches were his worst complaint after a double tour in the desert, he really had no complaints at all.

Dad's dream is gone.

Callie steered the car into the drive, angled it between the catalpa tree and Tom Baldwin's classic Chevy, then headed inside, determined to put on a happy face despite what just happened. The smell of Dad's stew reminded her of how often her father had been there for her, supportive, honest, caring and nonjudgmental.

Returning that respect was imperative now.

The men trooped in, their footsteps heavy on the back porch. Callie pulled out a loaf of fresh-baked Vienna bread crusted with sesame seeds, placed it on the table and settled a plate of soft butter next to the bread, her mama's custom because cold butter seemed downright unfriendly.

Right now a part of Callie felt unfriendly, but not to Dad and the guys. Or Jake, her beautiful son, her one gift from a sorry attempt at marriage to a fellow soldier.

Hank dropped a hand to her shoulder. She looked up, sheepish, knowing he'd see through her thin attempt at normalcy. "It's okay, Cal. He's young. Looks competent. And he must have the numbers behind him because the bank signed off. Those homes need someone now, not next spring when things might look better for us."

He was right, she knew that; she'd been handling his books for three years, and truth be told she did as well with a nail gun as she had with an M-16 and a computer spreadsheet, but—

"The important thing now is to save the houses. I'm hoping Matt Cavanaugh and his crew can do that."

She nodded, not trusting herself to speak.

Hank had personally planned that subdivision to honor her mother, the name reminiscent of her mother's childhood home along the shores of Lake Ontario, the quaint family cobblestone a salute to artisans of old. Hank had been determined to carry that classic neighborhood warmth throughout Cobbled Creek, his plans lying open on a slant board he'd erected at the back of the family room. He didn't glance their way now, and neither did she, the thoughts of all that time, effort and money gone in the blink of an eye, a slash of a pen.

Hank lifted the stew pot onto the center of the table. Tom and Buck grabbed bowls, napkins and utensils, the old-timers a steady presence at the Marek homestead. Jake put The General on the back porch and shut the door. He ignored the dog's imploring whine and triple tail thump, a sure sign The General would rather be curled up on the braid rug alongside the coming fire, but the smell of wet dog didn't rank high on Callie's list.

An engine noise drew her attention to the north-facing kitchen window.

Matt Cavanaugh's black truck sat poised at the end of Cobbled Creek Lane. Sheeting rain obscured her vision, but something about the truck's stance, strong yet careful, imposing yet restrained, reminded her of the man within, his shoulders-back, jaw-tight stance just rugged enough to say he got things done. His dark brown eyes beneath short, black hair hinted Asian or Latino, maybe both, his look a mix that defied the Celtic last name. She'd faced him almost eye-to-eye in three-inch heels which put him around five-eleven, not crazy tall, but with shoulders broad enough to handle whatever came his way.

She refused to cry, despite the disappointment welling inside. Stoic to the end, she'd been practicing that routine for years now.

Too long, actually, don't you think?

Callie pushed the internal caution aside. Survivors survived because they manned up, took the shot and stood their ground. Four years in the military taught her how to draw down the mask, put on the face, pretend disinterest as needed.

"Great bread, honey. Thanks for picking it up."

Callie turned, flashed the men a smile, laid a gentle hand on Jake's shoulder and nodded. "You know I'll do anything to keep you boys happy. Any word on when this storm's going to let up?"

Jake took her lead, such a good boy, so much like his grandpa. "Supposed to be nice tomorrow, Mom."

"Perfect." She smiled, ruffled his hair and sank into a seat alongside him. "We've got to finish the front of the house while we can, get it cleaned up so we can decorate for Christmas. We'll save cleaning the gutters—"

"Again?"

Callie sent Jake a "get serious" look and nodded. "Yes, again, they're filled with leaves and maple spinners. You know we can't leave them like that for winter."

"We don't want ice damming that porch roof again," interjected Hank.

Tom took up the thread, his face saying he'd play along, pretend everything was all right. "I remember Callie up on that roof last winter, luggin' that smaller chain saw, cutting through the ice."

"Bad combination of events, all around," agreed Buck. "To get that much snow, then warm up just enough to get a quarter inch of ice. Rough circumstances."

"But nothing we couldn't handle," Callie reminded them all. She'd used the short chain saw to hack through the pileup, pretending she didn't recognize the risk of being on a roof bearing thousands of pounds of unwanted ice, chain saw in hand. The roof's shallow slope helped steady her, but that flattened slope caused the initial problem, the lack of height allowing snow to gather and drift beneath the second-story windows.

"Exactly why we used steeper roof pitches on the subdivision," Hank reminded them. His expression said he was determined to face this new development like he handled life, head-on. "Quick water shed is crucial in a climate like ours."

"It is, Dad."

"Right, Grandpa."

Mouths full, Buck and Tom nodded agreement,

pretending all was well, but Hank's old buddies were no fools. Faced with the new realization that Hank's dream was in someone else's hands just beyond the big front window, Callie was pretty sure that nothing would ever be all right again.

Chapter Two

"What do you mean you've got no crew?" Matt asked his roofing subcontractor the next morning. "I can't do a thing until we get these places under cover with good roofs. We've got water-damaged plywood to replace, it's November and I need the crew you promised today. Not next April."

Jim Slaughter, the owner/manager of Slaughter Roofing and Siding sighed. "I'm tapped out, Matt. Fewer housing starts and reroofs. I'm filing for bankruptcy restructuring and hoping I can keep my house so we're not tossed out on the street. I had to let the guys go."

Matt's marine training didn't allow temper tantrums or bad vibes, even though he was tempted. "Who else might be available?"

Jim went silent, then offered, "You've got the Marek family right there, and Hank is friends with Buck Peters. They've all done roofing."

Ask the guy whose dream got yanked out from under him to finish that dream for someone else? Matt didn't have the callousness to do that.

Did he?

Matt eyed the farmhouse across the way. A ladder leaned up against the front. While he watched, the woman came out of the house with a bucket. She climbed the ladder, the unwieldy bucket listing her to the right until she settled it on the ladder hook. She pulled out a large green scrubbie and began washing the faded paint systematically, until she'd extended as far as she could, then she climbed down, shifted the bucket and the ladder and repeated the process despite the cold day.

A scaffolding would be so much easier. A power washer? Better yet.

He clenched his jaw and shook his head internally. "Another option. Please."

"I've got nothing. Literally. There aren't a lot of roofing contractors close by and making time for your job would be hard with a clear schedule. For anyone with jobs lined up, getting yours in would be next to impossible and a lot of people let their crews go from November to March because of the holidays and the weather. I was hoping to hold out, but the closing took too long."

It had, through no fault of Matt's. Bankers didn't comprehend weather-related restrictions and rushed work meant shoddy work.

Matt didn't do shoddy. Ever. He inhaled, eyed the house across the street and released the breath slowly. "If I get help, can you crew with them?"

"If it means fighting my way out of this financial mess, I'll work night and day," Jim promised.

"Can we use your equipment?"

"Absolutely."

Matt made several futile phone calls, carefully avoiding people who wouldn't give him the time of day for good, if old, reasons. And while plenty of construction workers were laid off, most had left the area, unable to survive on nonexistent funds. Half the remaining subcontractors were the type Matt wouldn't trust with his hammer, much less his livelihood, and the others were too busy to take on a huge project like Cobbled Creek.

Matt eyed the Marek place again and squared his shoulders, determined to find another way. He took two steps toward his truck, then gave himself a mental slap upside the head.

Jim made two very important points earlier. Was Matt willing to risk his investment on the possibility of bad workmanship?

No. His intent was to implement the appealing design plan that drew him initially. Of course it was less than beautiful now, and that had steered other developers clear. But Matt saw the potential and was determined to watch this pretty neighborhood spring to life under his guidance.

But rot problems would continue if the homes sat unroofed for another winter, and in the Allegheny foothills, rough weather came with a vengeance. He could complete inside work between now and spring, but outside endeavors were dictated by conditions. Lost time meant lost money, an unaffordable scenario to a guy who'd just invested a boatload of his and Grandpa's money into this venture.

He pivoted, then headed across the front field, his gaze trained on the house facing him, uncertainty and determination warring within.

Callie strode into the house after her lunchtime waitressing stint and came to an abrupt halt when she saw Matt Cavanaugh seated at their kitchen table, sipping coffee like he was an old friend. A heart-stopping, good-looking old friend.

Except he wasn't.

"Callie, Matt needs some help."

Callie bit back a retort, trying to separate the tough-as-nails guy before her from the situation that wrested her father's dream out of his hands.

Nope. Couldn't do it.

She moved past the table, set a couple of plastic grocery bags on the counter and headed for the stairs. "I'll leave you men to your discussion."

"It's a family decision, Cal."

Callie swallowed a sigh, one hand on the baluster, her feet paused, mid-step, then she shielded her emotions and faced them, albeit slowly. "About?"

"I need a work crew for roofing," Matt explained. His deep voice kept the matter straightforward and almost a hint detached, as if this wasn't about as insulting as life could get because he was talking about roofing *their* homes, *their* dreams, *their* project. "Jim Slaughter's run into bad times, he had to let his crew go and you guys know how crucial it is to get these houses roofed."

Hank nodded. "It broke my heart to see them sitting unprotected. Uncovered."

Callie knew that truth firsthand; she'd lived, breathed and witnessed her father's depression. His Crohn's disease had contributed to the ruination of what could have been a beautiful dream, a feather in his cap. She'd prayed, promised, cajoled and bullied God and this…

She swallowed a sigh, eyeing Matt, trying to look beyond the tough-guy good looks, the steel gaze, the take-charge attitude so necessary in a good contractor.

But right now this man represented their failure through no fault of his own other than being fiscally sound at the right time. While she couldn't hate him for that, a part of her resented his success in light of her father's failure.

A pessimist sees the difficulty in every opportunity; an optimist sees the opportunity in every difficulty.

Churchill's quote stuck in her craw. She crossed the room, poured a cup of coffee, moved back to the table, sat and eyed the two men. "I'm listening."

"Matt's offered some good money if we can crew alongside Jim Slaughter while his business is restructured."

So Jim's company had succumbed as well, and he had a nice, hardworking wife and two kids. Callie choked down a sigh. "Good money as in?" She turned Matt's way, keeping her affect flat, her gaze calm. Extra money was worth getting excited about for a combination of reasons, but taking it from the victor who now owned the spoils?

That cut. Nevertheless, her twenty-five hours of waitressing offered small monetary respite, not nearly enough to get by on, and she'd crewed for her father and his construction friends for years after leaving the military.

Matt's calm expression went straight to surprise. "You crew?"

And there it was, old feelings rubbed raw, his look reminding her of her ex-husband's disdain, how Dustin found her unfeminine and unappealing. She met his gaze straight on. "Yes."

The bare-bulb wattage of his grin should have come with a warning label. Sparks of awareness flickered beneath her heart, but she'd served in the military for four years and good-looking smiles had been a dime a dozen. But something about his...

"Well, that's an unexpected bonus."

When she frowned, he explained, "Numbers-wise. I knew your father was experienced, and his friend Buck, but to have a third person." He raised his shoulders in a half shrug. "That's clutch in roofing. And Jim Slaughter will help, too, so that makes five of us."

"Six, actually."

Matt turned back toward Hank.

"Tom Baldwin might be on in years, but he's a solid roofer. I know that firsthand."

"Excellent." Matt swept Callie another quick smile, just quick enough to make her want to shift forward.

Therefore she pulled back. "Except I haven't said yes."

"That's true." Matt stood, his shoulders filling the tan T-shirt beneath a frayed brown-plaid hooded flannel, the plain clothes adding to his hard-edged charm. "Here's my number." He handed her a business card, reached across and shook her father's hand, his frank gaze understanding. "Can you let me know by tonight?"

"Of course." Hank stood and walked Matt outside. "Let me talk to Buck and see if he's available. Tom, too."

"And, sir…" Matt hesitated, then turned, his eyes sweeping Hank, then the subdivision across the road. "I know this is difficult," he began.

Hank cut him off. "Things happen for a reason, son. Always did, always will. I can't pretend I wasn't disappointed by my run of bad luck, especially because it affected more than me."

Callie knew he'd shifted his gaze her way, but she kept her eyes down, not ready to rush this decision, although seeing Matt's grin on a regular basis wouldn't be a hardship. No, she'd definitely go to delightful. Maybe even delicious. But seriously off limits.

Like you're all that much to look at in hoodies and jeans with a tool belt strapped around your waist? Step back into reality, honey. Been there, done that. Bad ending all around.

"But I've wound 'round God's paths all my life," Hank went on, "the ups and downs, the back-and-forths, and we've always come out okay in the end."

"Good philosophy," Matt noted. He moved across the side porch, then down the steps. "I'll look forward to hearing from you."

"I'll call," Hank promised.

Callie stared at her coffee, not wanting it, not wanting to be broke, not wanting to work for the attractive guy across the street who seemed bent on getting them involved in his success while facing their loss.

"It's a good opportunity, Cal." Hank laid a hand on her shoulder, his gentle grip understanding.

"The location's convenient."

"Yes."

She sighed and stared out the window, seeing nothing. "And the money's good."

"And welcome."

"I'll say." She paused, drummed her fingers along the table top, then slanted her eyes to his. "I know we have to say yes, Dad."

He winced, then shrugged, understanding her mixed feelings.

"But I have to recount the reasons why before I do it."

"Like bills to pay?"

"For one." She nodded toward the school bus lumbering down the road. "I spent my Christmas budget on school clothes and supplies for Jake. He grew so much this summer that nothing fit, so I had to totally re-outfit him."

"And my little stash went toward truck engine repairs."

Two relatively minor things had dissolved their meager savings. Callie hated that, but then gave herself an internal smack upside the head.

Jake was strong, healthy and athletic, a good boy who loved traipsing off to a fishing hole, who behaved himself in school and accepted the necessary extra tutoring with little argument. He knew his way around a hammer and saw, a Marek trait tried and true, and wasn't afraid to don a hard hat and be a crew gopher.

Her father's health had returned with his colostomy, and if he continued to do well, they'd be able to reverse the procedure mid-winter. And while his appetite waned occasionally, she couldn't deny that good old-fashioned hard work was the best appetite builder known to man, and that getting back to work was in her father's long-term best interest.

The General dashed off the porch to greet Jake, his fur blending to grays in pursuit, the flash of white tail fringe the kind of welcome any boy would love.

"But the needy will not always be forgotten, nor the hope of the afflicted ever perish."

The words of the ninth Psalm flooded her, their comfort magnified in simplicity.

Callie liked things simple. She loved the feel of crewing on a house, walking scaffolding, climbing ladders, working a rooftop. Her father had affectionately called her his "right-hand man" from the time she was big enough to eye a square alongside him, and they'd laughed at the expression.

But you stopped laughing when Dustin walked out, citing your lack of femininity as a total turnoff.

Jake's dad had tossed her over for the former Livingston County Miss New York entrant, a petite gal who'd promptly given him two daughters in their suburban home in Rhode Island, neither of whom Jake had ever met. Dustin made it abundantly clear that his first family was an anomaly in an otherwise perfect life, therefore best forgotten.

Jake's entrance stopped her maudlin musings. She stood, smiled, grabbed him in a quick hug, then examined the papers he waved her way. "Another hundred on your math test?"

His grin said more than words ever could.

"And a plus on your homework sheets." She ruffled his hair, nodded toward a plate of cookies and the refrigerator. "Grab a snack, there are fresh apples in the crisper. I'm heading out front to get more of that mold washed off."

"Can we work on my science project tonight?"

"Absolutely." Halting her work on their home's western exposure for dinner, dark and homework left her little time to make progress, but Jake's enthusiasm over schoolwork outranked everything. His excitement came after years of grueling practice, nights when he hated her, mornings spent crying, not wanting to get on the bus because school proved too difficult.

"Success is not final, failure is not fatal: It is the courage to continue that counts."

Churchill's words uplifted her, World War II a favorite study topic for Jake, and having served in Iraq, Callie understood war rigors firsthand. While hyped battles might gain more press, small battles, fought daily, wore down the enemy, except when the enemy came from within.

She pushed that thought aside, refusing to revisit old feelings that should have abated long past. Sure, she'd been dumped. Callie was adult enough to handle that. But Dustin dumped Jake, too, and despite prayer and her best efforts, what did she long to do?

Give her ex the quick kick he deserved for abandoning a God-given miracle. The first gift of Christmas. A child.

But Callie refused to dwell on Dustin Burdick's shortcomings, although that proved harder at holiday time. She was home, safe and sound, with a beautiful son, a warm house and good friends. What more could she need?

The sound of a generator drew her gaze across the street. A light winked on in the model home, the only home near completion, and she caught sight of Matt Cavanaugh trekking back and forth from his truck to the pretty Cape Cod house, lugging things inside.

She pulled her attention back to the task at hand and climbed the ladder with her bucket and thick, green scrubbie, determined to get as much done as she could despite the chill, waning light.

Determination. Valor. Perseverance. She had the heart of a lioness and the grit of a soldier, two things vital to soothe the scarred soul of the woman within.

Chapter Three

Matt recognized Hank Marek's name and answered his phone quickly, praying for a "yes."

"We're in, Matt."

Thank you. Matt breathed the thought heavenward, knowing what even a day's delay could mean this time of year. They'd already been hammered by squalls packing hail, wind and rain. Time was of the essence.

"Everything's being delivered tomorrow morning," Matt told him. "I started roof examination today, but my day got chopped by having to order supplies."

"We'll be there at eight," Hank promised. "Callie works the lunch shift in town, but she's got Wednesdays off, so we'll have her all day tomorrow."

"What about Thursday?" Matt asked, assuring himself it was strictly a job-related inquiry.

Yeah, right.

"She'll split things up. She'll crew with us, then the diner, then back here."

Matt knew how abbreviated days curtailed time

frames, but did his frustration stem from Callie's prior commitment or...

No.

He refused to go there. Callie would be working for him. Matt didn't mix business with pleasure, no matter how intrigued he was by soft brown hair and gold-green eyes.

"That's her job," Hank continued.

It didn't take good math skills to realize roofing paid more, but Matt liked people that honored their commitments. His mother forgot she had a child when the world discovered he was Neal Brennan's illegitimate son. He was eight years old when life capsized. His mother sought solace in a string of random men, while his stepfather found comfort in a bottle. That left no one around to raise an eight-year-old kid with learning problems. Jake's age, he realized.

"But Buck and Tommy are available whenever. With respect to Tom's age I wouldn't put him on the tallest roofs, but he's sure-handed and has a good eye. And quick."

"He's welcome, then. Anyone else you can think of, Hank?"

A moment's hesitation followed, then Hank offered, "Your um—" indecision lingered in the older man's voice, his tone "—father's in town."

"Stepfather, you mean."

"I guess."

Matt didn't blame Hank for sidestepping the issue. When your biological father turns out to be the wealthy but drug-using, gambling vice-president of a local big business, Walker Electronics, the poor guy who'd been publicly emasculated took a hard hit. Don Cavanaugh became the classic definition of deadbeat dad, but because he *wasn't* Matt's dad, Matt guessed the expression didn't apply.

But it hit hard when the guy you called dad for eight years walked away and never looked back because of biology. That hurt, big time.

"He crewed with me a few times when I really needed help," Hank explained further.

"Then you know he's fairly unreliable on a day-to-day basis."

"When he's drinking, you're right. He's sober right now."

Sobriety was temporary in Don Cavanaugh's life, a hit-and-miss condition Matt would rather miss. "I can't trust him."

"Then I won't mention this when he's around. He'll notice when you change the sign, though."

"How?" Matt's father had no reason to be this far out of town and he hated the cold and snow. He'd race to Florida once the weather turned just like he had years ago, leaving Matt with his drama-queen mother.

Face front, eyes forward. No flashbacks, got it?

"Don comes by for coffee and soup with the other boys from time to time."

Which meant he'd see them working on Matt's new project, and the inevitable face-to-face meeting. "I can't have him over here, especially right now. I've got to get my bearings for this job. Find my comfort zone."

"I understand."

"Thank you, Hank."

"See you in the morning."

Matt disconnected the call and walked outside the house, eyeing the gloaming shadows beneath a waning gibbous moon.

A noise drew his attention to the Marek place. In the almost dark he saw Callie's silhouette, captured by the porch light. She clambered down the ladder, a bucket in hand, its weight making the descent awkward. At the bottom she splashed water onto the street, then headed for the side porch, humming.

Pride and strength embraced her maverick beauty. The idea of working for him obviously bothered her, but if she was as experienced as Hank made out, he was glad for the help.

Lights blinked on in the front of their house and he caught a glimpse of Callie and the boy, heads bent, eyeing something, a family moment that resurrected all he'd missed as a child. A father's love. A mother's touch.

He headed into the nearly complete model home, studied the mattress and box spring on the floor, the small generator outside giving him power for minimal light and heat. He'd surrendered his apartment in Nunda because the commute would eat up too much time. And saving nearly seven hundred dollars a month was nothing to take lightly. Wear and tear on the truck, his equipment? That took their toll over time.

No, better to headquarter himself here, on the job site, guarding his investment.

The house wasn't certified for dwelling, so Matt would have to sequester his sleeping arrangements when the inspector came by, at least until he could get a certificate of occupancy on the model. He'd complete that once the roofs were in place on the other houses, his first-things-first mentality key to this situation. Then he'd set up properly upstairs, but for the moment, this would do. He set his alarm clock early to take a shot at bookkeeping, not one of his strongholds, and burrowed under the covers, burying dreams of heat. And a woman with gold-green eyes.

"He's staying over there." Callie jerked her head west, her hands plunged into soapy dishwater the next morning.

"Makes sense," Hank replied as he gathered their tool belts and supplies. "Why pay rent when you've got a nearly finished house?"

"Because Finch McGee will be all over that if he finds out," Callie replied. She wiped her hands, waved goodbye to Jake as the bus approached, then headed to the table.

"Finch is a little power-hungry," Hank admitted.

"A little?"

Hank shrugged. "He's got a job to do, Cal. You know that. He just does it with more zeal than most."

"Maybe Matt will be lucky and Colby will be his

inspector." Colby Dennis had taken the job as Finch's assistant two years before, and he was a decent guy on all levels. Finch?

Callie'd been privy to more than one run-in with the divorced building inspector, and she knew a jerk when she saw one. She'd kept him at arm's length, but he'd taken to coming into the diner at lunchtime lately, when he'd always eaten at the Texas Hot before. And it wasn't a fluke that put him in her section, day after day, any more than it was coincidence that she traded tables with the other servers, keeping him at bay.

"Finch won't let the new kid on the block oversee this." Hank shifted his gaze to Cobbled Creek as they headed down the stone drive. "And while his inspections are all right, he doesn't have a lick of common sense when it comes to balancing economics."

"Ready, guys?" Buck grinned at them, crumpled his coffee cup and set it inside his truck cab.

"I am," declared Tommy, a knit hat drawn over his bald head, a thick flannel layered over a turtleneck.

"You expectin' a blizzard, Tom?" Hank teased.

"I'm expecting it's cold now and warmin' up later," shot back the older man, "and I've crewed with you often enough to know that cold and number of hours don't mean all that much."

"I knew I liked you." Matt smiled as he approached the group. "Supplies are due to arrive in three hours and Jim Slaughter should be here anytime with his equipment. Hank, can you get these guys together on inspecting the roofs, marking any part that needs to be redone while I finish a few phone calls?"

"I'm on it."

They spent the first hour setting up ladders and scaffolding, then split into two groups, checking for damage.

"We've got a problem here," Callie called out mid-morning as Matt passed by below. He clambered up the ladder, saw what she'd uncovered, and grimaced. "We'll have to take this section back down to the rafters."

"I'm on it."

She'd been amazing and quick, working hard and long beside the men without a break, and in her hooded sweatshirt and loose-fit blue jeans, no one would even know she was a girl.

So why couldn't Matt get it off his mind? *Focus, dude.* "You really have to go to the restaurant tomorrow? No chance of getting someone to cover you?"

Callie looked up. Had he tempted her? Heaven knows he tried. She shook her head. "Sorry, can't be helped. But I'll see if one of the girls wants to pick up my shifts next week because working here pays better than waiting on the lunch crowd at the Olympus."

"If you can do that, lunch is on me every day next week."

"For all of us or just the pretty girl?" Tommy wondered out loud.

"Everyone." Matt shot Tommy a quick grin of appreciation as he jerked a thumb in Callie's direction.

"Although she's easier on the eyes than the rest of you lugs." He headed back toward the ladder, the crew's work ethic easing his concerns. "I've got a friend who works at the Tops deli in Wellsville. She can hook us up with some pretty good eats."

Tommy exchanged a grin with Buck. "I had a few of those friends back in the day."

Matt laughed and discovered it felt good to laugh with a crew like this, as unlikely as they appeared. A gray truck turned into Cobbled Creek Lane, the town emblem emblazoned on the cab doors. Matt swung onto the ladder, his features relaxed.

Callie stepped toward the roof's edge, then squatted alongside him as though checking something. "It's Finch, the building inspector."

Matt paused his descent and nodded, wondering how the scent of fresh-sawn wood could smell so agreeably new and different to a longtime contractor like himself. Or was it her strawberry-scented shampoo?

"You're not from around here, but he's a little high on himself."

Relief tweaked Matt. She obviously didn't know he'd grown up here a long time ago. He chalked it up to their four or five year age difference. The old Matt Cavanaugh was best left forgotten, although that wouldn't be completely possible. He'd messed up big time back then. Now?

Now it was his turn to make things right. Make Grandpa proud. His newfound peace with his half brother and half sister, Jeff and Meredith Brennan, was a good start. Glancing down, he swept the gray truck a quick look. "Overzealous?"

"Bingo. And you can't let him see you have stuff in the model, that you're staying here."

"How did you…? Never mind," Matt continued.

Of course she'd notice, she lived across the street. His truck had been there all night and his lights were on before 5:00 a.m. "I'll steer him clear."

"Five-hundred-dollar fine," she muttered under her breath. "No contractor wants to waste a cool five hundred."

She was right. He'd traded off the apartment to save money, not throw it away. He climbed down the ladder, nodded his approval at the scaffolding Matt rigged in front of house number seventeen and stuck out a hand to the inspector. "Matt Cavanaugh. Nice to meet you."

"Finch McGee." The guy looked around amiably enough, but Matt hadn't tap-danced his way through the marines. Friendly snakes were still snakes, and Hank's daughter had this one nailed. That only made him wonder why, but he'd ferret that out later.

"I examined the initial plan when it came before the zoning commission." Finch surveyed the half-done houses with a thin-eyed gaze, then rocked back on his heels. "I wanted to give myself an up-to-date visual. You've got the copy of town code my assistant gave you?"

The demeaning way he said "assistant" tightened Matt's skin, but he tamped that down and sent McGee a comfortable look of assent. "Yes. How much leeway do I need with your office to set up inspections?"

"Forty-eight hours should do it. We're not slammed right now."

Not slammed? Talk about an understatement. The town had been literally asleep for the past eighteen months. But Matt heeded Callie's warning and gave in easily. "Forty-eight hours it is."

"You've got Hank Marek helping you?" Finch turned Matt's way. His approving expression insinuated that having Hank working on this project was some kind of power-hungry badge of glory. "Gutsy."

"Necessary." Matt clipped the word, needing to get back to work. "Hank knows this project inside and out. Who better to have on board?"

Finch shrugged. "Just seems funny, but no worse than hanging out in that farmhouse watching this place get ruined."

"Well, it's in good hands now," Matt told him, ready to cut this conversation short. "Mine and Hank's." He wasn't sure why he included the older man in the statement, but realized its truth right off. Despite hard times, Hank Marek was unafraid to put his hand to the task, a guy like Grandpa, tried and true. That kind of integrity meant a great deal to Matt.

"Nice outfit, Callie."

Matt turned in time to see the wince she hid from McGee as Callie came down the ladder.

McGee's words pained her, but why would a pretty girl like Callie Marek be hurt by a little teasing?

Two thoughts came to mind. Either Callie'd been hurt before or McGee's words came with a personal tang.

"She's working for you?"

Matt turned, not liking the heightened interest in McGee's tone but not willing to make an enemy out of the building inspector who would be signing his certificate of occupancy documents. "Yes, they're a talented family."

McGee acknowledged that with a nod as he headed out. "They are. I'll stop around now and again, see how things are coming along."

Translation: I'll stop around now and again to see Callie and maybe find you cutting code.

The latter insinuation didn't bother Matt. He refused to shirk and never used slip-shod methods in building. That had kept his reputation and business growing heartily in the northern part of the county. Now back home in the southern edge of Allegany County, where teenage bad choices dogged him, he'd be choirboy good to erase those dark stains on his character.

But realizing McGee would be stopping by to check Callie out?

That scorched.

And while Matt knew Callie was off limits, the way his neck hairs rose in protest when Finch McGee eyed her said his heart was playing games with his head. The way she'd faced the decision of crewing with him, upfront and honest, the way her hair touched her cheek, the brown waves having just the right sheen, like newly applied satin-finish paint…

Words weren't his forte, but feelings…those he got, and since he was fresh out of a relationship with a woman who'd wanted to change every single thing about him, he wasn't ready to charge head-first into another one, especially in a place where everyone knew his name and all the baggage that went along with it. With an employee. Nope. Wasn't going to happen for a host of good reasons.

"If you can trust yourself when all men doubt you, but make allowance for their doubting, too…"

Kipling's famous poem soothed the angst McGee stirred up, the poem a gift from Grandpa back in the day. Matt had to trust himself. He couldn't afford mistakes or missteps. He'd already made his share.

"Matt, you wanna cut those sections we removed or have me do it?"

Matt turned, grateful for Buck's interruption. "Have at it, Buck."

Buck nodded and swung down the ladder. "Be right back."

Matt climbed back up, inspecting each seam before they added the underlayment and the shingles. A mistake now would cost time and money later, every builder's nightmare.

Do it once, do it right.

By the time Matt glanced at his watch again, it was nearly one o'clock. "Hey, guys, lunch."

Hank waved a sandwich from the roof across the street. "Got mine right here, boss."

Tom did the same thing.

Buck straightened and rolled his shoulders to ease

muscle strain. "I'll bring mine up so we can keep going here. You want something, Matt?"

Their dedication touched Matt's heart. He'd worked with a lot of crews over the years, good and bad, and from both ends of the spectrum as low man on the totem pole and supervisor, but this…

He cleared his throat and nodded to Buck. "I've got a sandwich inside the truck. And some of those snowball cupcakes."

"I love them," Buck declared.

"Bring the box, we'll share. And see if the other guys want some."

"Hank won't. Coconut bothers him since he got the Crohn's, but Tom will dig in. So will Callie. She loves chocolate. Thanks, Matt."

"You're welcome."

Callie headed across the roof just then, a soldier's satisfaction marking her gaze, her walk.

A really good-looking soldier.

With great hair and pearl-soft skin.

Stop. Now.

He couldn't afford to mess up this job. He'd seen the careful way Hank handled his daughter, although this woman didn't seem to need protecting.

The image of her quick wince revisited him, the way she'd cringed at McGee's teasing, and that brought back another Grandpa Gus-ism. "If you respect women, you'll respect life."

Maybe Callie Marek *did* need protecting and was good at hiding it, but either way, she was off limits.

Her warm voice reenforced that notion a short while later. "Jake's home."

A yellow bus rolled toward them, lights flashing. Jake climbed down the steps, let the dog off the porch, then hurried their way with The General racing alongside. "You guys got a lot done today!"

Matt grinned as the pair drew closer, their enthusiasm contagious. "We did, but it's easy with a great crew."

"I can help." The boy's excitement made it tough for Matt to say no, but—

"We'd love your help," Callie told him, staving Matt's refusal with a sidelong glance. "First, get changed. Put on proper gear including your boots and hard hat, then head over here. There won't be much time, but you can work on cleanup."

"Okay."

The kid dashed across the open lot at a run, the dog streaming alongside, his pace pretty solid for an eight-year-old. Matt turned Callie's way, disapproving. "I—"

She held up a hand to thwart his argument. "I know what you're going to say, but trust me on this. Jake understands construction sites. He's been working side-by-side with us for years with no harm, no foul. He's great on cleanup duty and this is a much better choice than television or computer games, right?"

"Yes, but..." Matt met her gaze, decided that was dangerous because her eyes made him remember how lovely she was, even in roofing gear, and he didn't want to go there. No woman in her right mind would find his teenage police record a good thing to have around an impressionable kid like Jake. A *good* kid, Matt reminded himself. "Doesn't he have homework?"

"Yes." Callie nodded, chin down, focusing on her work, talking easily. "But he's got some processing problems so school doesn't come easily. We'll do it together, step by step, after supper."

That's what they'd been doing last night, Matt realized. "After working here all day, you'll do homework duty at night?"

She gave a brisk nod. "Of course."

He'd have given anything to have a mother like that. He'd tackled educational difficulties on his own and failed miserably. "That's amazing, Callie."

She turned, surprised. Their eyes met.

She went still, her eyes on his, her mouth slightly open, the parted lips looking very approachable.

And she read his gaze, his thoughts. It was there in her slight intake of breath, the way she blinked, the quick flex of fingers as realization struck.

Amanda Slaughter created a welcome diversion by pulling into the tract with promised coffee.

Matt was pretty sure he didn't want to be diverted.

Callie turned toward the ladder, breaking the connection. That was good, right? Neither of them had the time or energy to put into that quick flash of recognition. Obviously they'd be smart to ignore it.

But he caught her shifting a surreptitious glance

his way moments later, and that confirmed what he'd been struggling with all day.

Working side by side with Callie Marek meant he couldn't ignore her. And the over-the-shoulder look said she wasn't oblivious to the spark of attraction.

But a kid like Jake deserved to be surrounded by the best examples possible. Matt had been anything *but* a good example for a long time. Sooner or later Callie would discover his past. No self-respecting woman wanted a guy with a record setting an example for her kid, and Matt understood that. Respected it, even. He needed to remember he was in the southern sector of the county for two things only: to make amends to those he'd hurt and help Cobbled Creek become what Hank Marek meant it to be.

And although he was thrilled by the skill level and dedication shown by Hank and his crew, no way, no how was he looking for anything else. Especially where Callie Marek was concerned.

Chapter Four

McGee's truck reappeared while the crew grabbed coffee from Jim's wife. He braked quick, scattering stone, then climbed out, strode their way and met Matt's gaze head-on, his expression taut. "You living here, Cavanaugh?"

Matt's face showed surprise, not a good thing, but Hank's quick reaction spared a clash. "Of course he is, Finch. Wouldn't make sense to travel back and forth to Nunda while daylight hours are scarce, winter's closing in and every penny he's got is invested in Cobbled Creek."

"You don't have a C of O," Finch barked, his typical attitude more evident this afternoon. "There's reasons we've got regulations, Cavanaugh, although you were never real good at following rules, were you?"

Matt's flinch surprised Callie, but then Hank sighed and frowned as if wondering what the clamor was about. "Finch, I don't know any rule that says Matt can't live with us while he gets the model done and inspected. It makes good sense, all in all." Hank

kept his voice easy and his surprise genuine, as if taken aback by Finch's intrusion.

Callie swallowed a lump in her throat the size of a small two-by-four. Live with them? Was her father kidding?

"He's staying at your place?" Finch swept Callie a look, then drew his gaze back to the two men.

Hank shrugged, sidestepping the truth. "We have extra room. Matt needs to be on site. It works out for everyone."

Everyone but me, Callie wanted to shout. She was having a hard enough time keeping her distance from Matt in the short time they'd been working together, but to have him staying at their place?

"A perfect solution," Matt added, as if everything was suddenly hunky-dory. "And just so you know, I'm ordering us a fresh turkey for Thanksgiving."

Finch scowled.

Hank grinned.

Tom covered a laugh with a cough.

Callie decided more coffee would only tax her already-twining gut and headed back to the roof, trying to untwist the coiled emotions inside.

Yes, she was attracted.

No, she shouldn't be.

And having him under their roof, sharing their home, their food?

Way too much proximity and she had too much to lose, but Hank had extended the invitation and Hank Marek carved his word in stone. He kept a General

Patton quote framed on his dresser: "No good decision was ever made from a swivel chair."

Great. Just great.

Finch would be annoyed, which meant he'd annoy others. She'd have Matt underfoot which would entail having her guard up 24/7. And the guys were clearly delighted with the prospect of having Matt around, his friendly grin and storytelling a welcome addition to their circle, a perfect match.

But she'd found out the hard way there were no perfect matches. Not for women who strike a different path, a career that includes tool belts weighted with claw hammers and tape measures. Nails and utility knives. Unfeminine suspenders to distribute the tool weight appropriately.

Some lessons a girl never forgot.

Matt's footsteps followed her. He crouched by her side, pretending to work, his gaze down. "Hey, if it bothers you that much, I'll just get a place in town. Or stay at my brother's house in Wellsville. That way I'm not breaking the rules and McGee won't have anything to complain about."

Finch would dog Matt's steps, Callie knew. He wasn't above pestering contractors he didn't like, and he'd had his eye on Callie for the last several months. She'd kept it cool and friendly at the diner, but Finch added another component in an already-complex puzzle. She didn't want Matt targeted by the zealous building inspector, but she didn't want him living with them either.

Nevertheless, the invitation had been extended,

and Hank wasn't a man to go back on his word, a quality she shared.

She bit her lip and swallowed a sigh. "It's fine. It just came as a surprise."

"I'll do my own laundry."

His earnest words almost made her smile. "You bet you will."

"And I can cook."

"Excellent."

"How big a turkey shall I get?"

"You weren't kidding about that?" She turned to face him and felt the draw of those deep, brown eyes, tiny hints of gold sparking warmth and laughter. "I got a couple of frozen turkeys at Tops while they were on sale. That's a lot of good eating at a bargain price. Fresh birds are expensive."

"Have you ever tasted one?"

She brushed that off and turned back to the task at hand. "Turkey's turkey."

He grinned and moved a step away. "It's not, but I'll let you discover that next week. And now—" he shifted his attention back to the nail gun "—we need to get back to work. Can you help your dad and Buck get started on number twenty-three?"

Across the street and two houses up. Just enough distance to calm things down. Smooth them over.

"Sure."

"And Callie?"

She turned at the ladder and arched a brow, waiting for him to say more.

He eyed her a moment and shifted his jaw. "You do good work."

His awkwardness told her he meant to add something else but thought better of it. Just as well. Too much fun and teasing could be misconstrued. She headed down to ground level, crossed the street, moved up the block and joined her father on the elongated roof covering the well-designed ranch house. Hank noted her presence with a welcome smile and nod.

"Ready?"

Ready for roofing?

Yes.

For having Matt's teasing smile, his easy manner, his firm jaw around every day?

No way.

But Callie had withstood basic training and a deployment in Iraq. She could handle this.

She adopted a noncommittal look and started handing her father shingles, pushing thoughts of Matt aside, but with the steady pop of his nail gun keeping time with his whistling, she was mostly unsuccessful. Luckily no one knew that but her.

He'd be moving in tomorrow.

Ignoring Matt's light proved impossible as Callie helped Jake recognize consonant–vowel patterns for his language arts class. Her chair faced the front window, overlooking Cobbled Creek and the unshaded reminder of Matt's existence.

Change chairs, her conscience scolded.

She could, she supposed, warm yellow light pouring from the uncurtained windows of the model home. But...

"Mom, can I help Matt this weekend?" Jake asked, pulling her attention away from cute guys and broken dreams, definitely in everyone's best interest.

"We'll all be working this weekend, as long as the weather holds," Hank told him. "Your mom has a couple of shifts at the diner—"

"I switched them up with Gina," Callie cut in.

Hank eyed her, speculative.

"I make more crewing and we have no guarantee on the weather this late in the game," she explained to Hank, then turned her attention back to Jake's word list. "Yup, short *I* words here, long *I* there. Perfect."

Jake beamed. "Mrs. Carmichael told me to picture them like puzzle pieces, looking for clues."

God bless Mrs. Carmichael, Callie breathed silently. Between Hannah Moore's tutoring and Jake's teachers, he'd come a long way academically, and since his ADD prognosis, his continued progress thrilled Callie. She knew strong middle school academics required a solid foundation now, and she'd worked extra hours to pay for his tutoring, his book club, his interactive educational games, anything it took to surround him with learning opportunities.

So far, so good.

She smiled, ruffled his hair, tried not to glance out the window and failed, then said, "Yes, you can help, but The General can't be over there all the time, okay? We can't have someone's attention diverted when they're on a rooftop."

"Okay."

"And I want to get those Christmas lights strung this weekend. Thanksgiving's next week and I'd rather do it before we get big snows than after."

"That's a good idea," Hank agreed. "If we use both ladders we can do it together and get it done in half the time."

"True." The ladders were about the only thing not seized when Hank's business bellied up. The bank had considered them household use instead of business inventory. "I want to finish scrubbing that side, too. Get rid of the mold."

"Not much sense if we don't have time or the right temperature to paint," Hank told her.

"It looks better when it's clean." Callie didn't elaborate, but something about coming home to that worn facade weighed on her. Painting could wait until spring, but decorating for the holidays with the front of the house looking tired and worn…

That didn't sit right.

"When can we get our Christmas tree?" Jake's eagerness refused to be contained.

Callie laughed and stood. She stretched and fought a yawn. "Let's tackle Thanksgiving first, okay? And decorating the front of the house."

"Can we put up Shadow Jesus?"

Hank exchanged a grin with Callie. He'd created a plywood Holy Family years ago, the images of Jesus, Mary and Joseph done in silhouette, then painted black. Two spotlights tucked into the grass bathed the cutouts in light at night, making their shadowed presence appear on the white house. The simple, stark visual was an eye-catcher for sure.

Jake had referred to the infant in the manger as "Shadow Jesus" from the time he could talk, a sweet memory and a good focus on the true meaning of the upcoming holy season. "Next weekend," Hank promised. "It doesn't take long, but let's get the outside lights up first."

Jake nodded, satisfied. "Okay. Good night, Grandpa."

"Night, Jake."

He was such a good boy, Callie thought as Jake headed upstairs to bed. She would never understand Dustin's cool disregard for his beautiful son, but then she hadn't understood Dustin for a very long time.

Maybe ever.

"He's doing fine, Callie." Hank drew her attention with a nod toward the stairs. "Don't borrow trouble."

"I know. It's just rough at holiday time, when most kids get presents from their dads. Visits. Cards."

"He's happy enough."

"But he wonders, Dad." When Hank went to speak, she held up a hand to pause him. "I know he's content, but it weighs on his mind from time to time. His birthday. Christmas. When they do father-son events at school and church. And those are the times when I could wring Dustin's neck for brushing him off."

"And brushing you off."

She shrugged. "Not so much. We married young, we were both in the service, we thought we could conquer the world and when that didn't work, we grew apart."

Hank's snort said more than words ever could. "In my day skirt-chasing was called just that, and it didn't involve growing apart. It involved breaking vows, going back on your word. A good soldier never goes back on his or her word."

His righteous indignation struck a chord with Callie. "You're right, Dad, but it's in the past and I've moved on. We all have."

"And the future is ripe with possibilities," Hank reminded her. "Seek and ye shall find. Knock and the door will be opened unto you."

Callie leaned forward and planted a kiss on Hank's bushy cheek. "Are you letting your beard grow to keep your face warm on those rooftops?"

"Yes I am." Hank scrubbed a hand across the three-day stubble and grinned again. "One of the advantages of age and gender. I can grow my own ski mask."

Callie shook her head, laughing. "And I'm just as thankful I can't." She headed for the stairs. "I'm turning in early so I can work on the front of the house before first light. I'll turn on the small spotlights to help me see. Another few hours of washing should do it."

"If we had a power washer…"

Hank's quiet aside made her shrug. "We don't want to disturb the paint too much anyway. It's pretty loose in spots and a power washer might peel it off. Hand washing is fine for this year."

Hank hugged her shoulders and planted a kiss on her cheek. "You make me proud. You know that, don't you?"

She did. And she appreciated Hank's common-sense take on Dustin's behavior, but the image in the mirror once she climbed the stairs showed a strong, rugged woman, a laborer. And while her father's approval was a lovely thing, and Callie took pride in her work, her dexterity, her intrinsic knowledge of building, some days it would be nice to look in the mirror and have downright beautiful looking back at her, the gracious swan that evolved from the misunderstood fictional duckling.

But that wasn't about to happen.

Startled awake, Callie stared at the clock, rubbed her eyes and peered again.

She'd overslept the alarm. Not only would she not be scrubbing clapboard that morning, but she'd be lucky if she got lunches made before the bus pulled up for Jake. And what on earth was that noise?

Her father sent her an amused smirk as she ran down the stairs in her robe. "Tired?"

Grr.

Hank held up Jake's lunch bag. "We're good to go."

"Thank you." She gave him a half hug as she kissed his cheek on her way to the coffeepot. "I have no memory of turning the radio off or hitting the snooze bar. I must have zonked. And what is going on out there?" She jerked a thumb toward the subdivision.

Hank shook his head. "Not there." He pointed toward the street side of the house. "Here."

Here?

Callie followed the direction of his finger, pulled back the curtain and stared.

Matt Cavanaugh had brought over a small power washer. Using care, he splayed the jet of water against the siding in a slow and steady back-and-forth sweep, his attention locked on the task at hand.

"Pretty nice of him." Hank's words drew her gaze around.

"Very."

"Must have seen you working out there."

Callie was pretty sure the flush started somewhere around her toes and worked its way up. "Probably just wants to make sure we can use daylight hours on the subdivision."

"Most likely."

"Dad, I—"

She stopped as Jake clamored down the stairs, his expression a mix of surprise and delight. "Matt's washing the front of the house!"

"He is, yes."

"Then we can put up the Christmas lights this weekend!" He raced for the door and barreled across the porch, then down the steps and around the front. Callie watched from inside, pretty sure Matt couldn't hear a word Jake was saying.

It didn't matter. Matt's grin said he understood a

little boy's excitement. He nodded and sent Jake a quick thumbs-up as he guided the spray around the windows. He spotted Callie watching and for a quick beat he forgot to move the water wand.

Oops. His look of chagrin said he'd peeled a bit of paint.

He swept her one more quick look, barely noticeable except for the wink. And the smile, just crooked enough to be endearing.

Callie rolled her eyes, shook a finger at him and tried not to smile. She couldn't feed this flirtation and she had plenty on her plate dealing with Jake and Dad, but...

She let the curtain fall into place as Jake raced back in to grab a bagel and his lunch. "It looks great out there, Mom." He switched his look to Hank and raised both brows. "So we can decorate this weekend? Right?"

"When we're not working," Hank promised.

"Perfect." Jake gave Callie a quick hug and pointed toward the clock. "Matt says you've got fifteen minutes before you have to be at work and that you might want to get your coffee to go."

"Oh, he did, did he?"

Jake grinned and headed outside. "He's funny."

Funny. Right. She shooed Jake on. "Have a good day."

"I will." She heard him hail Matt as he headed for the road, The General at his heels, his voice upbeat. "See you later, Matt!"

She refused to check out Matt's reply, to see if he heard the boy's call.

She never overslept. Ever.

Her father poured a fresh cup of coffee into a thermal cup and swept her and the clock a look. "Twelve minutes and counting."

Laughter bubbled up from somewhere far away, a different kind of laughter. Sweet. Girlish. Kind of silly, actually.

But nice.

She hustled up the stairs, donned her layers and refused to think about the nice thing Matt was doing, saving her work, saving her time, precious commodities these days. And the joy in Jake's step…

That thought nipped the gladness. She didn't want Jake hurt. He'd taken a shine to Matt, but Matt was only temporary. If Jake grew too close…

Are you worried about Jake or you?

Both. Callie tugged her hoodie into place, grabbed a pair of fingerless gloves and headed back downstairs.

Matt's grin was the first thing she saw as she rounded the bottom step, his shirt cuffs damp from the sprayer, his hands wound tight around a mug of coffee. He flicked a gaze toward the clock, then back to her. "Right on time."

She faced him, tongue-tied. Despite her efforts, she couldn't get beyond that smile to create a quick comeback. And he saw that. Recognized the reaction. Probably because girls fell at his feet on a regular basis. His grin widened, lighting his eyes.

Not me, not now.

Callie grabbed her insulated coffee mug, not ready to play this game. Maybe she'd never be ready, and that might be okay. She headed out the door with Matt following, but as she passed the front corner of the house, she couldn't ignore what he'd done. She turned back and caught him studying her, his gaze curious. Maybe a little concerned. "Thank you." She waved toward the front and a hint of his smile returned.

"You're welcome."

"It looks much better."

He nodded, quiet, still watching her, one eye narrowed as if wondering something.

She pointed over his shoulder and slightly left. "Except where you peeled the paint above the window."

His smile deepened. Softened. He shrugged. "Distracted."

Talk about smooth.

Again the flush rose from somewhere deep and low, the pleasure of having a man flirt with her awakening sweet memories.

Memories that crashed and burned, honey. This guy's way cute, but he's here today, gone tomorrow. Let's not forget that.

She headed across the road, chin down, knowing he followed a pace behind, not hurrying to catch up. Was he waiting for her to come back? Match her pace to his?

Or just enjoying a walk with his coffee?

"House looks good, Matt." Buck smiled and nodded appreciation toward the Marek place as they drew alongside. "And that means we can rig up Shadow Jesus soon, I expect."

"And the lights," Hank added. "Jake sure is excited."

"I got that." Matt grinned, took a sip of coffee and settled an easy look Callie's way. "He's a good kid."

"Thanks. Same assignments as yesterday, boss?"

A muscle clench in his chin said he recognized the marker drawn. "Sure." He headed right while she moved to join her father and Buck on the roof they'd begun the previous day, but his light whistle followed her, the tune young. Bright. Carefree. It called to her but she'd put carefree aside a lot of years ago and it would take more than clean clapboards and perfect teeth to bring it back. Most days she was pretty sure it was gone for good.

So much for maintaining a distance, Matt thought as Callie headed across his roof on steady feet a few hours later. "Tom said you needed a hand over here."

Matt nodded, brisk, pretending immunity. "I do, thanks. The pharmacy called to say his wife's prescription was ready."

"And he didn't want her waiting." Callie adjusted her gloves, flexed her fingers and squatted beside him, close enough to notice how her lashes curled up on their own with no help from mascara. "That's Tom, all right. And since Dad and Buck are capping twenty-three, I was the logical choice. Looks good

Jim," she noted, raising her voice so Jim could hear. "And it's almost straight."

Jim made a face at her. "Ha, ha. Do I have to remind you that I've put on more roofs than anyone else in Allegheny County?"

Callie laughed. "Since there's no one here to argue the point, I'll let you stake your claim. In the meantime," she turned her gaze toward Matt.

"Do you want to feed or nail?" he asked.

"I'll nail. Then we can switch so neither one of us ends up with a backache later."

"And you didn't leave for the diner today. How about tomorrow?"

Callie shook her head, eyes down, working the nail gun as they edged right. "Nope."

Matt fought off the quick glimmer of appreciation her answer inspired. *Focus on your work. Remember that you're on a rooftop and concentration might be in everyone's best interest.* But he'd be lying to say that Callie wasn't a pretty nice distraction, totally against the norm of women he'd known.

"I switched with Gina," she continued, working as she talked. "She's a single mom, too, and she can use the extra shifts. She'll do doubles, which will help her out at this time of year."

"Christmas."

"Christmas and winter clothes," she told him as she shifted her angle to give him more room. "With kids you go right from back-to-school clothes to winter clothes and then Christmas. There's no such thing as saving a dime in the fall. Not with children."

Tom's truck pulled back in a few minutes later. He climbed out, surveyed their progress and whistled, appreciative. "Nice work."

Matt grinned, showed a thumbs-up and jerked his head toward Hank and Buck. "Can you finish up with Hank and Buck?"

"And let you have the pretty girl all to yourself?" Tom drawled. He tipped his wool hat toward Callie, ever the gentleman. "Good thing I'm a happily married man. I might be giving you a run for your money."

Matt shook his head, pretending indifference, but when he glanced Callie's way, twin spots of color brightened her cheeks.

The wind, he decided.

"Ready here."

He started feeding her shingles again, her speed and concentration commendable when it was all he could do not to notice how she moved, the way she handled the nail gun as though born to it, her manner decisive, her gaze intent, her lower lip drawn between her teeth as she squared up each section.

She didn't talk, she worked, and Matt appreciated that. Talking slowed things down, and they were already racing the clock. Callie understood the time line and stayed focused on the job at hand while Matt had a hard time focusing on anything but her.

A car pulled up. Amanda climbed out, toting a

drink tray of fresh coffees from the convenience store at the crossroads.

"She's a lifesaver," Callie muttered from behind Matt.

Matt met her gaze and smiled. "I'll say. Now if she only thought to bring doughnuts..."

Amanda set the tray of large coffees down on the saw table tucked inside the garage of number seventeen, then headed back to the car and pulled out a big box of doughnuts.

"No wonder he loves her."

Callie laughed out loud, Matt's easy humor a comfortable draw. "And times aren't easy for them."

"Exactly." Matt nodded her way, before tilting his gaze toward Amanda. "But they go the distance. That's why I contracted Jim initially, but the closing took weeks longer than expected and he was already treading water."

"Tough business climate for builders," Callie noted as she climbed down the ladder ahead of him, pretending not to notice how nice he looked from behind in his jeans, his movements sure and steady. A guy who looked that good in denim ought to be doing TV commercials.

This is a work relationship, it's money in the bank, Callie. It's a chance to get through this winter in the black, instead of the red. You can't afford to let anything mess this up.

She knew that, but couldn't deny the pull. She'd been a soldier for years. A good soldier learned to assess and acclimate, then decide.

She'd assessed Matt, all right, and she was tempted to get a little more acclimated, but when it came to the decision-making part of things, she had one job first and foremost: to take care of Jake and her father.

She couldn't afford to tip this job into negative territory, and romance gone bad could do just that.

Nope, she'd be friendly, work hard and hope Matt kept them on as he proceeded to finish the homes her father had started.

Matt turned and handed her a coffee. Their eyes met. He stood, holding the coffee, her hand skimming his, their gazes locked, electrifying the moment.

"Cream?" He half choked the word, then rolled his eyes, smiled and leaned forward, his voice soft. "I don't think my voice has broken like that in nearly twenty years, and I was talking to a pretty girl that time, too."

Callie accepted the coffee, slanted him a wry glance and reached for two little creamers. "Twenty years between girls? That's so not normal. You get that, right?"

He grinned and added sugar to his coffee before sidling her a look. "Maybe it depends on the girl."

"Makes men choke." Callie nodded, stirred her coffee, put the lid back on to help ward off the cold and turned his way. "I'll put that on my list of attributes if I decide to go on one of those internet dating sites."

"Or you could spare yourself the trouble and just

go out with me." The look he sent her said he was only half-teasing.

An offer she'd love under different circumstances. She'd figured that out when she'd found him sitting at their kitchen table, firm but at ease, decisive, but kind when pushed to ask for their help. Matt's warmth and self-confidence spelled "good guy" in bold letters, but this good guy was also her boss.

"I never date the boss," she told him, keeping her tone easy but her answer firm. "If things go bad it makes for a rough work environment."

His look said he agreed but wished he didn't. He handed her the open box of doughnuts and indicated them with a glance down. "May I offer you first choice in doughnuts at least?"

She grinned, wishing she could have said yes to going out, but glad he recognized the dangers, too. "That's quite chivalrous of you."

"The least I can do, ma'am." He tugged his wool hat slightly, the maneuver endearing, but Callie couldn't risk endearment.

Could she?

Not when he controlled the paycheck.

Chapter Five

~~❦~~

Callie walked into the familiar setting of the Jamison Farmers' Free Library for the weekly fundraising meeting that evening. In partnership with Walker Electronics, the towns were raising funds to upgrade and expand the tiny library tucked in the vintage village. Callie loved being on hand to help raise money for the good cause because Hannah Moore, the former librarian, had tutored Jake the last two years, inspiring him, laughing with him.

And now Hannah was engaged to Matt Cavanaugh's brother, Jeff Brennan, her cochair on the library committee. Which meant Callie couldn't stop thinking of Matt while seeing Jeff and Hannah.

But she was having a hard time not thinking of Matt without Jeff and Hannah around, so tonight wasn't much different than every other night this past week.

"Callie." Hannah sent her a quick grin of acknowledgment and handed off meeting minutes from the previous week. "Do you mind setting these around for me?"

"Glad to." Callie laid a copy on each chair while Hannah finished measuring coffee.

"Done."

"Me, too." Hannah crossed the room and grasped her hands. "Hey, I wanted to say I'm sorry about your father's subdivision. It's got to be hard, watching it being developed right across the street from you."

"Actually…"

"We all know how hard you worked on it…"

Callie grasped her friend's hand to shush her. "Hannah. Pause. Breathe. Dad and I are still working on it."

Hannah frowned. "Huh?"

"Matt hired us to crew with him."

Hannah's frown turned into surprise. "Gutsy move. Not like that should surprise me." She sent a wizened look toward the door as Jeff walked in, looking confident and happy to see his future bride. "They are brothers." She refocused her attention on Callie as Jeff paused to talk to Melissa, the young woman taking over Hannah's job at the library. "Are you okay with all this?"

Callie's hesitation outed her.

"Oh, honey." Hannah made a face of concern. "You don't have to work for him, you know. Not if it's that hard."

Hannah had clearly misunderstood her pause in conversation. As Jeff moved into their area, Callie hedged. "It's fine, really. Matt's amazing and we're already making great progress on the houses. And that's good for Dad, mentally and physically."

"Glad to hear it." Jeff slipped an arm around Hannah, planted a soft kiss to her hair, but kept his attention on Callie. "And I told Matt he could stay with me, but he said he was going to finagle a spot onsite because he can't afford to lose time with the short days now."

"And that's a fact." Callie didn't mention that Matt had moved into their extra room, and that his burly presence added a whole new dimension to their home. That his laugh shook the rafters and his smile…

Oh, that smile…

Luckily other committee members began trooping in, saving her from making a complete fool of herself. Jeff moved off to greet people, but Hannah stayed put. She swept Callie an up-and-down look before nodding. "Hmm."

Callie frowned. "Hmm?"

"Hmm."

Hannah tossed Callie a knowing look over her shoulder as she set pens around the table. Callie shook her head, firm. Resolute. "No hmms. Strictly business."

"I know exactly what you mean." Hannah jerked a thumb toward Jeff in the crowd of new arrivals. "A few months ago I was fighting tooth and nail to get off this committee. Now I'm marrying my cochair. Oh, I get it, Cal."

"I barely know the guy," Callie protested.

Hannah leaned closer, grinning. "I think that must be one of their special gifts, honey. And I can't say

I'm a bit sorry. But because they are aggravating, industrious, somewhat know-it-all men…"

"With a great sense of humor."

Hannah acknowledged that with a brisk nod. "Call me if you need me. Or if you just want girlfriend time."

"Aren't you busy planning a wedding?"

Hannah laughed and lowered her voice as others approached. "Dana took over."

Callie grinned. Jeff's mother was well-known throughout town, a pillar of the community, a stalwart, God-loving woman unafraid to get dirty or put her hand to any task.

"Leaving me free to teach science." Hannah tipped another smile Callie's way. "And see my fiancé."

"Perfect."

"It is." Hannah gave Callie's hand a light squeeze. "And Matt, well…" Her smile deepened. "Dana raves about him, and I'd trust her opinion on anything. I'm just getting to know him myself, but he seems like one special guy."

Callie didn't need that reminder. Still, it was nice to see the approval and appreciation in Hannah's eyes because Matt was sharing their home, their food, their table. She faltered, then dropped her gaze to Hannah's hands, Hannah's soft skin tweaking her. "Do manicures help?"

"Help?"

Heat rumbled up from somewhere deep inside Callie. Not that she cared about what her hands looked like, but soft skin, pretty nails…

"My hands take a beating," she confessed. As committee members started to settle into seats, she held up her hands. "Construction work is tough and this cold, dry weather isn't exactly friendly to the skin."

Hannah tilted her head, smiled and winked. "You need a little Meredith time."

Callie frowned. "Jeff's sister?"

"Jeff's sister ran a posh spa in Maryland until a month or two ago. Let me set up an appointment for you."

Callie shook her head. No way could she justify spending money on a frivolity like that when cash was so tight.

"And don't worry about the money," Hannah added as if reading her mind. "Meredith's a sweetheart and she'll do it just to help her brother's friend. We can do it at Dana's place. Or mine."

"Um…"

Hannah's laugh said she realized she'd railroaded Callie and didn't care. Callie had never met Meredith Brennan, but she knew Hannah. Trusted her. She had a hard time imagining people spending hard-earned money on fancy nails, a true skeptic when it came to anything construed as froufrou.

Except a great pair of heels. Those she understood.

The press of committee members pushed her back into meeting mode, a good thing when talking about Matt just made it easier to think about Matt. Better for both of them to keep him out of sight, out of mind.

And definitely better from a paycheck perspective.

* * *

"I think the rain will shut down roofing tomorrow," Matt announced the next evening. He set two bags of groceries on the counter and laughed when Jake zeroed in on the Christmas tree snack cakes.

"I love these!" Jake exclaimed, eyes wide. "Mom, can I—"

"First, no, it's too close to supper. And second, they're Matt's, not ours."

"Rule number one," Matt said. "Any food I buy is up for grabs."

"Sweet." Jake mimicked Matt's grin and Matt high-fived him like they'd put one over on her.

"Still, not before dinner. Either of you."

Matt sent her a look across the room, a look that said more than words. He gripped Jake's shoulder and nodded toward the homework table. "If you've got homework, I'd be glad to help."

"Sure."

"He's been here two days and already he's replacing me?" Callie asked Jake, a hand to her heart, feigning hurt.

"That way you can have some downtime after supper," Matt advised. "Maybe we can play Yahtzee. Or UNO." He scanned the game shelf. "But watch out if you take me on in war." He pumped up his chest and drew his shoulders back. "Me being a soldier and all."

"Mom was a soldier, too," Jake chattered as he pulled his agenda and binder out of his book bag and laid them on the window table. "So was my dad."

Callie kept her wince hidden, but something about Matt's analytical gaze said he saw too much. He carried the discerning air of a marine, and while that should be a comfort, Callie didn't need anyone discerning too much. Not now, not ever.

She lifted the soup pot lid and breathed deep before spearing a carrot. "Almost done, so you guys have about fifteen minutes. Because I've been replaced, that is."

"Only temporarily." Matt flashed her a teasing grin, but his words reminded her this was a short-lived setup, not a permanent convenience.

She'd tried ignoring him for the first twenty-four hours he lived there.

Fat chance.

Then she tried treating him like a brother.

That didn't even come close to working.

Friends, she decided that morning. Good friends.

They'd worked side-by-side all day and now had only two houses left to roof. With Thanksgiving approaching, the guys would need time to be with their families.

The weather forecast didn't look great, and each day meant the odds against them were growing. They needed two solid days, maybe three of decent weather.

God, please, asking you to govern the weather seems a little bossy with all you've got going, but please... Help us get these last two homes covered.

"If it's raining we can install windows."

Matt nodded, pointed out a problem to Jake and turned her way. "Exactly what I was thinking. That way we don't lose time and prevent further damage. And the Tyvek wrap will help keep external walls from getting damaged over the winter if we can't side them right away."

Not getting them sided would disappoint him. He'd laid out his plans the first night in their house, showing the time line to Hank and Callie after Jake had gone to bed.

Hank had eyed the plans and made a skeptical face. "It works if everything goes perfectly."

"Exactly."

"So if it doesn't," Hank continued, turning a frank look Matt's way, "We prioritize. Roofing. Tyvek. Windows. Get them sealed as best we can. Then interior work over the winter won't suffer damage."

"And with a four-month window to get the Tyvek covered," Matt observed, "we can apply siding when the weather starts to ease."

"Yes." Matt's respect for the manufacturer's guidelines earned him Hank's approval. "Warranties remain in effect and the town doesn't cite us for not following code." Hank's expression changed as he realized what he'd said. "You, I mean. Not us."

Matt had offered him a straight look. "I wouldn't be here if it wasn't for you, Hank. Your vision. Your plans. Your project. Having you on board makes my life a whole lot easier right now. I'd be foolish not to realize that, and I finished being foolish a long time ago."

Matt's words eased her father's strained expression, and Callie blessed him for guarding the older man's ego. Hank's self-esteem had taken a beating these last two years, first from a debilitating and somewhat embarrassing illness that left him wearing a colostomy pouch, followed by losing the business he'd spent thirty years building. And because Callie had worked for Hank's company, the double loss of income spelled near disaster.

Matt's investment in Cobbled Creek changed all that.

His presence in their home was changing more than her business perspective, but she'd made a firm decision to keep her distance. Her father and son had been through enough, and adding romantic drama to an already-tense life would be foolhardy. Hadn't Matt just mentioned how he'd stopped doing foolish long ago?

Well, so had she, about the time Dustin walked out leaving her with an eight-month-old baby and little money.

Matt's engaging laugh drew her attention to the man and boy profiled in the window, heads bent as Jake worked out a word problem. Matt fist-pumped when Jake got the answer right, and Jake's answering grin reaffirmed what Callie had shared with her father the week before. Jake didn't know his dad enough to miss him, but he missed *having* a dad. That was evident in the shine he took to Matt, the way he tried to emulate Matt's moves on a house. If she wasn't careful, Jake would fall in love with the square-shouldered, sturdy builder and have his heart broken once Cobbled Creek was complete.

She couldn't let that happen, but she couldn't deny Jake the chance to hang with Matt, talk with him. Chat with him. Matt's positive influence was good for Jake. She recognized that. And while life handed out good and bad, some rough turns could be character-building. A boy didn't grow to be a man without scraping a few knees, and Jake was no exception.

"Done." Matt grinned at the boy, satisfaction lighting his face.

"Done." Jake echoed, exuberant. He glanced at the clock. "And we did it quicker than Mom does. She talks a lot."

"I do not."

Matt held his hands up in surrender, his eyes bright with humor. "I didn't say it." He jerked a thumb Jake's way. "He did."

"'Cause it's true," Jake added as he put his notebook away.

"She's mighty quiet on those rooftops," Matt noted as he withdrew plates and bowls for the table. "Hard to imagine her a chatterbox here."

Callie sent him a faux-withering look. "I talk as needed."

"And then some," offered the boy.

"Jake."

He laughed and dashed off to the living room to call Hank and Buck.

Callie eyed their study table and shifted her gaze to Matt as she piled biscuits into a napkin-lined basket. "He might be right. I tend to go overboard, always explaining. Showing him the whys and wherefores."

"That's not a bad thing." Matt took the basket from her, lifted it to his nose and breathed deep, appreciation brightening his dark eyes. "These smell wonderful."

She grinned. "Good change of subject."

"I do what I can, ma'am."

Callie paused, one hand reaching for the soup kettle, Matt's words and tone sparking a memory of life in the service. Soldierly reparté.

"You okay?" Matt gazed at her, puzzled, a brow thrust up.

"Fine." Callie shrugged, grabbed the soup with both hands and shook her head. "Just a déjà vu moment."

Matt set out spoons and butter knives like he'd been setting tables all his life, but the look he sent her was only half-teasing and not at all unappreciated. "Cal, trust me on this. If we'd met before, I'd have remembered."

She felt the blush rise from her chest, staining her face and neck, and despite her best military ways, she couldn't tamp it down. "Artful flattery, marine."

"Yes, ma'am." He smiled across the table as the older men lumbered through from the living room. "Two tours in Iraq taught me to plan for the future but live in the moment."

"Good advice, son." Hank nodded approval as he sank into the chair, breathing deep. "Cal, this smells wonderful."

"It does," Buck chimed in. "And I grabbed some ice cream this morning. It's in the freezer on the porch. I thought someone might like a sundae to-night." He targeted Jake with a grin of appreciation. "There's fudge sauce in the cupboard 'longside the sink. And whipped cream in the fridge."

Jake beamed. "Thanks, Buck. I thought you forgot."

"No, sir, I did not." Buck ladled his bowl of soup, set it down and passed the ladle on to Hank. "When this old soldier makes a promise, he keeps it and you worked hard to make that honor roll."

"He sure did." Hank smiled approval at the boy. "Hard work pays off. Got your homework done already?"

Jake waved toward Matt. "Matt helped me while Mom finished supper."

"Ah."

Her father's partial word said a lot, maybe too much, but Matt took it in stride. "The smell of this soup prevailed on me, sir. A good Marine does what he must to facilitate great food."

"Amen to that," added Buck. "And speakin' of amens, if you'd bless this food, Hank, we could commence to eatin' and I for one am mighty hungry after workin' rooftops all day."

Hank offered his typical short, clipped blessing and Callie sent him an "Are you kidding me?" look.

He grinned and dipped his spoon into his soup. "No need to look at me like that, daughter, I spent my day praying on that rooftop. God understands short and sweet as well as he does long and drawn out."

"Can't have the biscuits cooling off," Matt chimed in reasonably.

"Would be a cryin' shame," added Buck as he slathered butter across his. "Though Callie's biscuits are fine hot or cold."

"A good selling point," Matt noted, grinning.

"Yet totally unnecessary when nothing's on the market." Callie kept her tone light but directed a pointed gaze at Matt.

"Duly noted."

"Good."

"Did they come and switch up those shingles for number thirty-one?" Hank asked Matt, shifting the subject to Cobbled Creek, a change Callie welcomed.

"First thing in the morning. I'm glad you caught the mistake, Hank." Matt shook his head. "I can't believe I almost missed it."

"The three and the eight in the code looked mighty similar, but gray shingles in the midst of all these other homes?" Hank made a face. "That would have been bad. This way they're here in time and we don't waste a day. If the rain holds off."

"And I can be here only Monday and Tuesday next week," Buck explained, his tone reluctant. "We're headin' down to the daughter's place for Thanksgiving and won't be back until Saturday. Mother's got to have her shopping day with Jeannine while Bob and I hang out with the kids on Friday."

"Family time's important." Callie smiled at Buck, then shoulder nudged him lightly. "And you know you love wrestling with those boys."

"Though they're too big for that now," Buck admitted. "Tim's in sixth grade, and Tyler's a freshman in high school this year. Seems funny to have them that grown."

"Family is meant to be enjoyed," Hank assured him as he went back to the soup pot for seconds. "The good Lord wouldn't have it any other way."

Hank's choice of expression struck Matt.

Nothing in his family had been enjoyable. Hank's words shone a new perspective on his parents' choices. Neither one held any belief system holy or sacred, neither one invested time in anything but themselves. Matt hadn't known the warmth of a candlelit church service until Gus took charge of him, and it took the rough stint in juvie to put him back on track.

But he'd done it. Finally. With help from his beloved grandfather.

He felt Hank's gaze on him, measuring. Assessing. That single look said Hank knew his past and understood his present, and Hank wouldn't have invited him to live under their roof if he didn't trust him, right?

But Hank knew Matt's stepfather, which meant he knew the clutch of drama surrounding Matt's parents. The two fathers left a legacy of drinking, gambling and womanizing. It wouldn't be a big leap to wonder if Matt carried either man's hard-hitting characteristics. Half the town knew Matt had been headed full-bore in that direction as a young man.

He'd stopped that train of self-destruction, but folks had long memories. His past would intrude on the present, which meant he had to make the here and now as pristine as possible, no hassles, no hurries, no mistakes.

And sitting at the Marek table, Matt never wanted anything more.

"Uh-oh."

Callie peered at Hank as she shimmed a window from the inside while Hank and Buck adjusted the outside the following afternoon. "What?"

Hank jutted his chin toward their house, visible through the back opening. "Don's here."

Callie followed his gaze. "And that's bad because?"

Her father made a face, then pushed out a breath that sounded long overdue. "He's Matt's father."

"He's…" Callie paused, squinted toward the window, then faced Hank. "He's what?"

"Matt's father. Stepfather, actually. In a convoluted weird kind of way."

"You either are or you aren't," Callie corrected him. "It's a legal term. So, is he or isn't he?"

"Is he or isn't he what?"

Perfect. Just perfect.

Callie turned toward Matt's voice, mad at herself for talking about him when he wasn't there. Except he *was* there.

"Don's at the house." Hank pointed toward the road. "I was just explaining to Callie…"

"No sense explaining what can't be understood." Matt rubbed his hands against his jeans, two wet stripes darkening the denim. "I lived it and I still don't get it."

"I'll go talk to him," Hank said. He made a move toward the door and Matt caught his arm.

"I'll do it."

"But you said—"

"I know." Matt studied the view beyond the window, the older man climbing out of his truck, heading toward the house. "But there's no time like the present to have this said."

"You sure?"

Matt shook his head and made a face. "Not by half, but I'll do it anyway."

He strode out the door, climbed into his truck and drove the quarter mile, wind-whipped rain beating on his truck, the wipers slapping up and down in furious fashion. Callie turned toward her father. "I don't get it."

"Neither do I," Hank admitted. He turned his attention back to work. "But it's Matt's story to tell. I just happened to know some of it."

She sent her father an incredulous look. "You're not going to explain this?"

"Nope. Sorry. Gotta ask him."

That wasn't about to happen. She'd managed to keep personal conversations to a minimum so far and...

So far? You're on day five. Not exactly world record pace.

Oh, she got that. But it *was* significant because she'd fought off the inclination to share sweet banter with Matt, knowing he could get under her skin.

Worse, he recognized the ploy. She saw it in his gaze. The set of his chin. The tilt of his head, the tiny muscle that twanged now and again in his jaw.

Knowing his marine background and his patient demeanor, she'd sidestepped anything that might be of import conversationally.

But now, seeing him climb out of his truck and mount their side steps, she kind of wished she knew what was going on.

"I've got the rest of the windows unpackaged." Buck's voice interrupted her wandering thoughts. "Callie, you need help?"

"I'm good, thanks."

Buck stared out the window and then met Hank's gaze. "Uh-oh."

"I said the same."

Callie swept the pair a look of disbelief. "You both know what's going on?"

"Before your time, I expect." Buck helped Hank balance the living room picture window as they lifted it into place from outside. "Cal, can you give us a hand here?"

Callie helped leverage the lower edge of the window into the expertly cut opening. "Nice job, Dad."

"Thank you. And I'm still not telling you. A man's got a right to privacy."

"She could ask him herself," Buck supposed.

Like Callie needed to hear *that* again. "Or not."

"Suit yourself." Buck nodded approval of the window fit as Callie leveled it from inside. "Kind of nice to have an uncurious woman around. Refreshing, you might say."

Uncurious?

No way.

But she refused to feed the gossip mills at anyone's expense. The thought that Don and Matt were related shouldn't be a surprise with the same last name, but lots of Irish had settled into the lower counties of New York State. Cavanaugh wasn't exactly rare.

But she'd noticed the pained look that crossed Matt's face before he hardened his jaw. That flash of emotion said the past colored the present, and Callie understood that reality tenfold.

Chapter Six

"Matt." The older man's face paled when Matt strode into the Marek kitchen, giving Don an unhealthy hue. Not that Matt cared.

"Don." Matt kept his voice calm, his affect flat, and refused to use the term *Dad*. That title had been forever tainted in his mind by both men, but he was beyond letting their callousness affect the boy who lingered within. Most days. "No one's here right now."

"What are you doing here?"

"Working." Matt jerked a thumb west. "I bought Cobbled Creek from the bank. Hank and his buddies are helping me get things winterized."

Don lifted his chin, surprised. "You own Cobbled Creek?"

"Yes."

Don passed an aging hand across the nape of his neck. It didn't tremble. A good sign, Matt supposed. "Hank was hoping to buy it back himself."

Matt stayed quiet, his silence punctuating the obvious.

"You need help over there?"

A part of Matt's gut seized. Another part froze. Did the guy who walked out on an eight-year-old boy who'd known him as dad just ask for a job?

Matt conquered his instincts and shook his head, wondering if he could locate a punching bag nearby. "Got it covered, thanks. Hank's invited me to stay here." He waved a hand, indicating the house. "Until I get the model certified."

Don's expression hinted the sorrowed man within. But Matt had endured more sorrow than a kid should ever have to, so Don could just take his angst and—

"...forgive us our trespasses as we forgive those who trespass against us...."

The sweet words of The Lord's Prayer proved wickedly hard to follow right now. Matt would discuss that with God later, but for the moment... "I've got to get back to work."

"Oh. Sure." Don hauled his wet hat back onto his balding head with two hands. "I'll get on, then."

He'd put on weight. And lost hair. And his teeth could use work. Matt saw all that and tried to equate it with the guy who played catch with him in the backyard. Who took him to Little League games to cheer on the home team. Who promised him the world until the day he realized he had no legal responsibility for Matt and walked out the door, never to be seen again.

Old anger resurged, too sharp to be considered controlled.

But Matt managed it. As he led the way out, he

waved toward the subdivision again. "I expect this will take a while."

"I see."

Don's expression said he understood what Matt didn't say. *Keep your distance until I'm out of here.* He nodded. "Good luck on your project."

Matt refused to acknowledge that. He didn't need luck; he had faith. He didn't need handouts; he needed workers. And God himself knew that Matt didn't need a pretend father hovering on the outskirts of his life, one who should have been holed up in Florida collecting unemployment checks until spring.

If I was a father...

Whoa. Matt put the brakes on that train of thought in whipcord fashion. He carried enough bad genes to ruin a dining room table full of kids, so the idea of procreating?

Wasn't gonna happen.

Nope, he'd stop the craziness of passing on Neal's and his mother's self-absorbed genes right here. He had his work. His company. His service buddies. And a host of construction people in the northern section of Allegheny County admired him for his pledge of excellence and work ethic.

His brother, Jeff, and his new fiancée, Hannah, could produce the next generation of Brennan blood.

Guilt speared him as he approached 17 Cobbled Creek Lane. His grandfather had loved his Latino heritage. And he'd married an Asian woman who taught at a local preschool until her untimely death from ovarian cancer. Matt only knew her in pictures, but Grandpa's praise painted a rosy picture.

And his mother had been beautiful. But looks only go so deep, and if he had to hunt two generations back to find goodness in his family tree, that was too far. Being upfront about that saved a whole lot of wasted time and emotion.

He parked the truck, climbed out and ducked inside the house, damp chilled air surrounding him.

Comfort later. Work now.

That's how he got through the Corps. And through the early days of forging his own company. And through the lean times of project start-ups. He should be used to it by now.

"Need help over here?"

A new warmth stole over Matt. He turned.

Callie stood inside the door. She indicated the house across the street with a nod. "Dad and Buck have that one just about done and I figure we've got a couple of good hours of daylight left, even with the rain."

"Did you have lunch?" Matt didn't remember seeing her leave or eat, so...

"Work first," she told him, moving inside. "Plenty of time to eat once it gets dark and you stay warmer if you keep moving."

A part of Matt respected her stance. Another part wanted to bundle her in a blanket by a cozy fire and make sure she was warm. Fed. Comfortable.

Red alert. You've entered a "no cozy fire" zone. Proceed at your own risk.

"You're right." He headed outside as she moved into the great room area. "Let's see if we can get this done before Jake gets home."

Callie laughed. "He's spending the night at Cole's house, so I'd hope so. I figured that worked out well because we can't put the Christmas lights up in this rain. But maybe tomorrow."

Matt wanted to help with that. He wanted to see Christmas through Jake's eyes, the eyes of a beloved child.

"We'll make sure they go up tomorrow, one way or another," he promised. "I'm not afraid to get wet. As we're about to witness."

"Thanks, Matt." She smiled his way and the warmth that flickered when she walked in the door intensified. "I can manage the lights, but it's easier with two people."

"Yup. Hank and me. You can make supper, or something."

She sent him a "get serious" look as she unpackaged a window. "Keep the little woman in the house? Are you kidding me?" She flashed a glance around them. "You get what I do, right? Climbing a ladder to hang Christmas lights is no biggie."

"Even so." Matt double checked the window dimensions, snapped his tape shut and raised one shoulder. "It wouldn't hurt for you to be warm one day out of seven."

A spark of pleasure brightened her eyes, but she quenched it pretty quick. Not quick enough, though, and Matt wondered how long it had been since anyone had taken care of Callie. Treated her like a woman. Treasured her.

Seeing Don must have lit some emotional fire within him, a flicker of flame that better get squelched quick. He needed the Mareks to make his dream happen. They needed him and his paychecks to survive their current situation. No one on either side could afford to muck this up. So he wouldn't, plain and simple.

Although catching her gaze through the rough-cut window opening made him want to rethink his position.

Time to change the subject. "I figured church first thing. Then a few hours over here. Then Christmas lights and football."

Callie laughed out loud. "After the week you've put in, I'd call football well-deserved entertainment."

He winked in agreement. "Monday's weather looks clear. We can resume roofing then. And if we get this house enclosed by tomorrow night, we're better than halfway done."

"And making sweet time."

"Which brings me back to tomorrow's schedule."

Callie helped stabilize the window as he lifted it into position from outside. "Yes?"

"You in an apron."

She blushed, shook her head and slid thin wooden shims beneath the frame, eyeing her carpenter's level.

"With some kind of great Sunday afternoon meal going," he continued, raising his voice to be heard through the window and over the rain.

"An apron?"

He widened his grin and flicked her outfit a glance. "Saves wear and tear on your flannel shirts."

She didn't answer right away, and when he balanced the window and glanced down, she wasn't smiling.

"Hey, I was kidding. You can get your flannel shirts dirty if you want to. They're washable."

Something flashed in her face, the pain he thought he'd seen the week before, as if…

He had no idea, but he felt bad. And stupid. "Hey, Cal, you don't have to cook." Was her lower lip trembling?

No. She wouldn't do that, would she? Get girly on him?

"Actually, I'll cook," he added hurriedly, anything to put off the possibility of a woman's tears. Nothing in the Corps taught him how to deal with those, and that seemed downright wrong and maybe dangerous because he didn't know a male soldier that muscled up to a crying woman. "And put up the Christmas lights. And finish the windows. Just don't cry, okay?"

She scowled, blinked and shrugged, eyes down. "I don't cry."

Right. Matt refused to argue the whole shaking-lip thing. He knew what he saw, but God had also given him a working brain and arguing with an emotional woman? Not smart. "Well, good. So I'll cook…"

"I'll be glad to cook." She finished the shims, assessed the level, then whacked the excess shim board away with more energy than required. Like double that. "I like cooking. Occasionally."

Something wasn't adding up. "Then why the long face?"

"No long face." She straightened and sent him a reassuring look. "See?"

Oh, he saw all right. He saw a soldier that knew how to draw down the shield, a gallant woman who'd learned to quell emotion. And normally he'd praise that talent, a skill not easily attained, but here? Now?

He wanted to help. He longed to ease the flash of hurt and insecurity. Inspire her laughter. But seeing Don face to face left him fresh out of funny things to say.

Cut him some slack, Callie's inner voice advised. *That meeting with Don couldn't have been the easiest thing in the world.* And something she'd like to know more about at some point in time. But not now, when she'd already gone girly and emotional over an innocent comment about her work clothes that should have been funny.

But it wasn't.

Callie moved to the next window, then drew up short. "Oh, I forgot."

Matt checked the frame size before he looked up. "Forgot what?"

"You got a call on the house phone."

"Oh. From?"

"Reenie."

He sent her a puzzled look, one that almost looked

sincere, and it wasn't as if Callie cared who called him. Or what they looked like. How they dressed. Really.

"What did she want?"

"Does secretarial pay come with the job?"

He grinned, which meant she let too much emotion creep into her voice, a trend that occurred regularly around Matt Cavanaugh. "Under 'hazard pay' in the fine print. Better read your contract more carefully next time." He held the window in place while Callie leveled it. "So?"

Silent, she winged a brow through the glass.

Matt heaved an overdone sigh, playing along. "Did Reenie leave a message?"

Callie was tempted to pretend she hadn't, except because she had no vested interest in Matt Cavanaugh, why would she even consider such a thing? "That she's fine with next week and your cell phone was out of service."

He pulled out the phone, scanned his bars and made a face. "Signals get choppy down here."

"Sometimes. That's why we kept the landline. Something to think about when you get your C of O on the model." She bent low, then made a quick sure cut, her home-building confidence intrinsic.

Her self-confidence?

Whole other kettle of fish, but she wasn't going to get into that with Matt. Hopefully he'd chalk it up to bad timing or whatever. And she could care less who Reenie was.

Liar, liar, pants on fire...

She stood back as he positioned the next window, shushed the inner voice, then nodded approval. "I've always loved these house plans. Each one distinct despite the neighborhood similarities."

"That's what drew me to Cobbled Creek." Matt sent her a frank glance of approval. "Your dad has a great eye for manipulating design just enough to maintain a neighborhood feel but leave each house unique. And the hillside setting, leaving established trees in place." Matt's appreciation for the aesthetics raised Callie's confidence a notch. "A perfect draw."

Callie slanted up a knowing smile. "He had help."

Matt read her inference and grinned. "You?"

She nodded. "I love that kind of thing. Setting. Blending. Coordinating."

"Interior stuff, too?"

She shook her head. "Decorating's not my forte. But home design. Placement. Light filtration. And kitchen setup. That stuff I get."

"That's a gift, Callie."

"I know." She moved to remove the casing from the dining bay windows. "And Dad was never afraid to let me use it. I love that about him."

"So you do that with Jake."

"Is it obvious?"

He nodded. "Definitely. You draw the best out of him, but don't smother him. You let him find his way. That takes guts."

She shrugged, not wanting to explain too much, but grateful for Matt's compliment. "I want him to feel independent. It's hard for kids who need extra help in school. It gets embarrassing."

"It sure does."

His wry note drew her closer. "Don't tell me you struggled in school, marine."

"Ha." He moved to the east side of the house and measured, then remeasured before grunting satisfaction. "School came hard. That's why I think it's cool how you help Jake. Teach him. Coach him."

Callie heard what he didn't say, that no one had bothered to do that with him. Her heart pinched at the thought of his little boy struggles, how challenging it must have been. And yet he'd conquered those dragons. He must have, or he wouldn't be standing here today. "Somewhere along the way you caught up."

He winced. "Took too long. Wouldn't wish that on anyone, so you just keep doing what you're doing. Jake's a great kid."

The unspoken part of that comment said he hadn't been a great kid, and that quiet admission nicked Callie's work-hardened reserve a little more. "Thanks, Matt."

He didn't reply, just angled a look toward the far side of the window. "Can you catch this when I slide it into place?"

"Sure."

They inset and leveled the five tall, slim windows framing the dining space. When he finished setting nails in the last one, he grunted approval. "It looks good and it's getting dark. Done."

"I love the look."

She gathered tools and left the mound of wrapping. "We'll stow it all once we're finished with windows." They headed down the walk, then the stone drive. As they hit the road, Callie turned. "It's starting to look like something, Matt."

"It is." Matt's approving tone made her feel good, which was silly, really, and yet...

"Which one is your favorite?"

She didn't need to consider the question as they moved into the street. "The model, of course. That's why it's the model, it's the one I pictured living in. Hearth and home, classic Cape styling, paned windows, stone front." She turned and waved a hand to the rest of the street. "These are all good designs, but when I tweaked the model I tried to incorporate everything I'd love in a home, starting with the feel. The emotional response it creates in people."

"Women, mostly."

She laughed and bumped shoulders with him. "Probably, yes. But is that bad? What man doesn't want his wife to be happy? Or what woman wants to scrimp on the home she's worked for years to get?"

"But you kept it affordable." Matt paused and turned her way as they reached the Marek driveway. "That's a rare talent, Callie."

She started to shake her head, but he paused the action with a hand to her shoulder. "Don't shake me off. It's true. Especially now, with mortgage lending tight and housing needs tanking. You managed to make these homes something that invites investment, promotes families and is affordable. That took knowledge and a keen eye for placement. Thank you for that."

His words rang sweet because she'd adjusted the original plans for all his listed reasons, but gazing up into his eyes, those deep, dark pools of chocolate, his grateful expression put a hold on her heart. And her tongue. For the life of her, she couldn't wrap her brain around anything to say, not when he held her gaze and her shoulder, the strength of his grip something to lean into. Rely on.

"Callie…" His attention slipped from her eyes to her mouth, his expression wondering. Maybe hoping.

Callie took a firm step back, unwilling to wonder, not daring to hope, refusing to play in waters that nearly drowned her before.

Matt stood strong and silent, watching. Waiting. Giving her a chance to move toward him or step away, and despite how badly she'd like to take that first step in his direction, she moved back and quieted a sigh. "We had an agreement, remember?"

"I was hoping you'd forgotten."

"No, you weren't." Callie pulled her flannel closer and swept the subdivision a look. "We both need this done. You need to guard your investment, I need a paycheck. Dad, too. And muddying the waters would be ill-advised. Besides, the guys all kind of look out for me."

"Because your husband left you alone to raise Jake while he traipsed around with another woman?"

She smacked his upper arm and refused to feel

bad when he cringed in pretend pain. "Leave it alone. Please. And have you noticed that while I've guarded your privacy like an M.P. at the gate, you've managed to dig up half my life history? Level the playing field or change the subject."

"First, that's some left jab you've got there." He sent a look of overdone admiration to her left arm as they climbed the stairs to the side porch and rubbed his arm, pretending she'd really hurt him. As if. His corded upper arms were steel bands and looked mighty good in a T-shirt. Not that she noticed.

"And second," Matt continued, "I think it was the guys' way of issuing warnings. Letting me know they stand to protect you from other stupid men who don't appreciate how wonderful you are."

"I don't need protection." She made that pronouncement as they approached the door. Matt paused her with a hand to her arm again.

"What *do* you need, Callie?"

Need? Want? The list was too long to articulate, but she'd trained herself to keep things to a minimum. She leaned forward, just enough to let him think she was reconsidering the glance he'd sent to her mouth, then tapped him on the nose when he drew close. "A paycheck. And peace on Earth would be nice, too."

She stepped back, gave his knit cap a gentle tug and headed inside, leaving him to follow.

As she shed her outer layer of work clothes, the memory of that near kiss played with her heart. Her head. But she knew better than most what fickle things men were, so she'd keep herself focused on the task at hand. Home-building. Roofing. And while a little flirting might not be a bad thing, she couldn't risk upsetting this apple cart of opportunity.

"I'll start a load of heavy stuff."

She turned straight into one of those dull brown T-shirts he favored, muscled marine chest and shoulders straining the worn seams, the soft cotton fabric needing a good washing at the end of the day.

And he was still appealing.

She didn't need an air raid siren or blackout curtains to remind her she was in grave danger, but she couldn't quite remember the last time danger felt this refreshingly good.

Obviously she was food-deprived.

Hank saved the day by walking in with an extra-large pizza. Callie headed for the kitchen while Matt started the washer, the mingled scents of pepperoni, sausage and cheese replacing cotton knit.

But even after skipping lunch, there was no way Callie could fool herself into thinking the pizza smelled better than the well-worn shirt, and that spelled trouble.

Chapter Seven

❧

Matt studied the five church choices facing the park green, a sweet template despite the bone-chilling rain. And from the steady stream of cars rounding the circle and pulling into backyard parking lots, Jamison folk weren't about to be deterred by the seasonal drizzle.

What's your goal?

To pray.

Soldiers didn't need a church for prayer, but Matt wouldn't confuse Jake by staying home on a Sunday morning. He also wasn't about to go to Good Shepherd with the Mareks, not when so many people from his past were members.

He wasn't after confrontation, just peace and quiet. Solace.

He slid the truck into a parking space along Main Street, climbed out and approached the White Church at the Bend, second-guessing himself.

Maybe he should have headed north. Route 19 went straight to Houghton, a sweet college town with several churches, but that extra twenty minutes meant productive time wasted.

It also ensured privacy. Matt was less likely to meet his past on the streets of Houghton. Jamison and Wellsville?

The past met the present at every corner.

Man up, marine.

Matt entered the small church, found an innocuous seat on the far left and sat, eyes forward, determined to pay attention to nothing but the service.

The sound of dripping water thwarted his vow. A spreading damp spot encroached the plastered ceiling over the altar. The budding smell of mildew shouted wet basement.

And was that a taped-up electrical connection on the left?

The old place had seen better days. Flaking paint above the congregation meant damp wood. The floor was older than dirt and looked it.

The little church needed help, and a construction guy like Matt knew how quickly things went from bad to worse if left too long.

"Gettin' worn around the edges, ain't it?"

Matt turned toward the outside aisle. A small woman with a cane stood alongside his pew. Matt moved in to make room, and when she had trouble wrestling her cane into submission, he helped hook it on the pew's back.

She breathed a sigh of gratitude as she sank into the seat. "Thank you."

"You're welcome."

She nodded forward, then leaned back against the cream-colored pew. "You're in for a treat this mornin'."

"Am I?" Matt settled back and smiled. "Good."

"Katie's playin' for us."

"Ah." He nodded politely, ever the gentleman.

"Her father don't like that she comes here, but Katie ain't never been one to listen to his harping on this, that or the other thing."

Matt twitched inside. He'd come to pray, not catch up on local news, and he was just about to sidle right when a young woman entered the sanctuary area from the left.

Katie Bascomb.

Guilt power-washed his heart.

A C-clamp seized his lungs, the turning screw tightening with each breath.

His fingers went numb, the adrenaline rush pouring pins-and-needles energy into his extremities.

She looked lovely, and that beat the way she'd looked the last time he saw her. Broken. Bloodied. Bruised.

Memories blindsided him, images streaming like a bad video feed, showcasing what he'd done.

But mostly what he'd failed to do.

He started to leave, feeling certain he had no right to be here, invading Katie's life. Her time. Her peace.

The old lady leaned closer. "Do you mind helpin' me out when service is over?" She skimmed the cane and the rain a cryptic look. "I'm not as steady as I used to be. I live a few doors down Main Street. If it's not too much trouble," she added, as if asking for help pained her.

He wanted out, big time.

But he couldn't deny this grandmother's petition. "I'd be glad to, ma'am."

Her smile soothed a little. Or maybe it was God. Or memories of Grandpa Gus hugging his shoulder and saying, "We all make mistakes. Then we learn from them and go on. Or not." He'd nod and grip Matt just a little tighter. "The choice is ours."

Katie positioned herself in front of a stool. Two clips held her long, blond hair back from her face, a face that seemed too serene for what she'd suffered because of him.

A long, flowing skirt rippled its way to the floor in some crinkled material, a blend of bright fall colors vying for attention. An earthy necklace hung against a pale sweater, its chunky beads accenting the colors below.

She looked beautiful. And mature. And peaceful, a violin grasped in one hand, a bow in her other. She quickly glanced at the small but growing congregation as if teasing them, as if guarding some fun-loving secret from her vantage point at the altar.

Shame wrenched his gut because he knew that under the placid beauty lay a broken woman.

His fault. All his fault.

He had to leave.

A young couple with two small children edged into his pew from the right.

Blocked.

Unless he *wanted* to be noticed and he could guarantee that was the last thing on his to-do list that morning. Why hadn't Katie stayed at Good Shepherd where her parents had gone forever?

Sweet notes sang from the front, single haunting notes inviting prayer.

Right until they jumped into quick succession, the small congregation grinning as if in on the secret. Katie's hands flashed the bow across the instrument. As one, the congregation stood, keeping time, heads bobbing, wide smiles matching hers. Clapping.

Obviously Matt had landed in a place that *looked* like Jamison but became some sort of "sixties"-style Celtic fair once you walked through the double oak doors of the White Church at the Bend.

The old woman jutted his arm. "Ain't she somethin'? And our new pastor, well, he's got people comin' in to do all kinds of things now. Nothin' slow or easy 'bout his way of doin' things and I say good for him!" She punctuated her approval with a firm nod that looked almost grim. "'Bout time we had someone rile up this old church. Best we've been doin' lately is diggin' holes, settin' one after another to rest. Now we've got young families comin' in. Bringin' their babies." She grinned across him to where two preschoolers eagerly awaited whatever was going to happen next. "New life."

And that's what he wanted, wasn't it? Why he'd come back to Jamison? To atone for the old and make way for the new.

A young man wearing a black-and-gold football

jersey and wide grin strolled onto the small altar as Katie picked out a foot-tapping arrangement of "When the Saints Go Marching In."

The small crowd erupted, singing and clapping, welcoming the man despite his presence in the heart of Buffalo football fans. Matt grinned in spite of himself.

It took a gutsy guy to claim his team in enemy territory, but the young pastor's face said he'd handle whatever came his way. Matt liked him immediately, an uncommon occurrence for a marine.

By the time the atypical service concluded, Matt was sure of two things.

Katie was doing okay.

And Jamison had changed.

"Loretta, you've found yourself a new beau," the young pastor exclaimed as Matt assisted the aged woman out the back door once the life-affirming service had concluded. "And you're new here." The pastor clasped Matt's hand, grinning an amused welcome.

Matt swept the town a glance. "I grew up here."

"You did?" The old lady shot him a look of shrewd interest.

"Then you know how wonderful it is firsthand." The pastor pumped Matt's hand with an easy vigor. "A great place to settle down. Raise a family. Or come home to. Right, Loretta?"

"Yessir."

Because Matt wasn't inclined to do any of the above, he hedged. "Nice to have you here, Reverend."

"Si," the other man corrected. "Simon MacDaniel, but everyone calls me Si."

"But you *are* a reverend, right?"

Si grinned. "Got me a nice diploma from one of those mail-order places to prove it."

"Oh, you!" Loretta's grin lit up her face, easing the chronic line of worry.

Matt grinned despite himself. "Then I should expect reggae next week?"

"I'll get Katie right on it," the pastor affirmed as he turned to greet the next person. Matt hoped Si turned quick enough to miss his reaction. As he headed down the front walk, commotion across the leaf-strewn park said his timing had gone awry.

The doors of Good Shepherd swung open opposite them. Either Reverend Hannity cut his sermon short or Si had waxed on. Matt glanced at his watch and made a face.

Si's fault, which made him a good preacher in Matt's book, but that proved small comfort as streams of people headed toward vehicles parked creatively here, there and the other place. While the five churches created a postcard-like ambiance to onlookers, the Sunday morning reality became a logistical nightmare, guided by a sheriff's deputy in rain gear, allowing traffic into and out of the circle.

Only in Jamison, Matt thought, but as confusing as the moment appeared, he found himself longing to belong. A huge part of his life had been lived in this town, like those unfinished houses he now tended.

He'd been rough-cut. Unpolished. Not plumbed

to fit anywhere, so he'd made up his own rules and crashed and burned, taking Katie and two of his buddies with him.

The guys had walked away with barely a scratch.

Katie hadn't walked away at all. Not for a long time, and then it took a prosthetic and loads of therapy. She'd been doing physical therapy while he did time, but in the end, he gained his release and walked free.

Katie was still missing a leg.

He longed to move quickly, berating himself mentally for not going to Houghton, but the aged woman's pace urged caution.

Jake ran their way, oblivious to the rain, a wide grin lighting his face. "Matt! Did you see this?" Waving Matt forward, Jake stopped in front of a large sign. "They're doing Christmas lights in the park! And sleigh rides! In the dark!"

Jake's voice spiked the exclamation points to new highs, his enthusiasm contagious.

"Looks fun, bud."

"A little pricey," Loretta noted.

Matt eyed the ticket cost and saw Jake's expression dim, but the boy didn't wallow or pout. He manned up with a stout smile and said, "It is kinda pricey and who wants to go see old lights anyway?" He turned a bright gaze up toward Matt, his earnest expression pulling Matt in. Brave. Stoic. Sturdy. What a kid. "And we're putting our lights up today, right, Matt?"

"Right. But let me get this nice lady out of the rain, Jake, and I'll see you at home."

He raised his gaze and saw Callie watching from the edge of the park green. A hint of winsome softened her smile, as if wishing… wondering…

Hoping?

Back off, dude. Would that pretty lady be looking at you that way if she realized what you had done? Who you were?

No way.

You there, God? I thought this was a good idea. I thought I'd come down here, make amends, fix things and move on. But maybe I'm being selfish. Maybe my presence will hurt more than it heals.

Matt passed a hand across Jake's head, escorted the old woman to her door, then headed back to his truck, eyes down, pretending oblivion.

"Cavanaugh."

Most civilians didn't realize how dangerous it could be to sneak up on a marine. Matt stopped himself from putting a hold on the middle-aged man, but just barely. "Mr. Bascomb."

"What are you doing here?"

Since Katie's father served on the town council, he knew why Matt was in town. Howard Bascomb had tried to nix Matt's zoning approvals for Cobbled Creek but couldn't, and that bit deep with the older man. Because Matt was responsible for what happened to Katie two decades back, he couldn't say he blamed him. Still… "Going to church."

"Katie's church."

Matt raised two hands, palms out, in surrender. "I didn't know that until she stepped onto the altar."

"Stay away from her." Howard took a step forward, his gaze menacing, but Maude McGinnity must have sensed something was up. She bustled through the door of the Quiltin' Bee, her sewing and quilt shop that pulled in tourists from all over. "Howard, good morning. And Matt." Maude reached out and gave him a hug, an obvious move meant to quell Howard's angst. "So good to see you. I hear you're doing some fine work up there on Dunnymeade Hill. We'll all be happy to see Cobbled Creek finished, Hank Marek most of all."

"Yes, ma'am."

She grinned and tugged him inside, leaving Howard in the rain. "May I show you something?"

"Yes." Matt elongated the word, reading her ploy. "And thank you," he added as Howard trudged in the opposite direction.

"You're welcome." She kept drawing him forward and Matt paused, puzzled.

"You really have something to show me?"

She frowned. "Yes."

"That wasn't just a maneuver to break up the drama on your front step?"

Her knowing smile confirmed his guess. "That, too." She led him into a room where racks of hand-sewn quilts were displayed away from the south-facing windows.

"Wow." Matt eyed the walled display, then the racks. He arched a brow and angled Maude a look of admiration. "Amazing work."

"My Amish women." She nodded, brisk, and

moved several poled quilts aside. "But this is the one I wanted you to see."

He stepped forward as she singled out a beautiful coverlet arrayed in a mix of quilted and embroidered flowers. "Mama's Flower Garden," she told him, a fond smile crinkling her face.

The blanket was a virtual backyard of color, tone and warmth, the three-dimensional feel of some of the blossoms a salute to warm, sunny days. The vibrant mix of hues heralded spring, and in the dank, gray days of November, spring seemed a long time off.

"It's lovely." He fingered the quilt again, then turned, puzzled. "But why are you showing me?"

"Hank Marek commissioned this for Callie before everything tanked. It was a Christmas present for her, but then he couldn't afford it, so I put it out here."

Matt flipped over the price tag and winced. "The most expensive one of the bunch, of course."

"Let's call it creative financing." Maude grinned at his hiked brow. "I didn't want anyone else to buy it, so I discouraged the purchase. Think half what you see and it's yours."

"Mine?"

"If you're interested, that is." Her facial expression read "all business," but the gleam in her eye said "yenta."

Matt took a broad step back. "Hank might want to get it himself."

"Possibly." Maude's look said she wouldn't push, but it also said she didn't think it likely that Hank could put together over five hundred dollars for a blanket.

Matt started to turn away, but reached out for one more touch. "He really commissioned this for her?"

Maude regarded the quilt, then Matt. "He said when Callie came back from Iraq, she was different. More subdued."

Matt could understand that. War could change people, but because women weren't allowed in combat, he didn't think the effect held true for them. Maybe he'd been a little simplistic in his assumptions.

"And that she missed color most of all."

That statement hit a note as well. The flat, dull tones of desert duty held none of the warmth and drama of Allegheny County, its beauty ever-changing in the dance of seasons. "That's true."

"Callie's mother loved to garden. She had a knack, that's for sure. That's why Hank picked this design." Maude flicked the quilt a quick, dismissive touch. "Well, you know it's here. That's really all I meant to do."

"And break up the confrontation with Howard."

She mulled that as she walked him out front. "Howard's not a bad person, but he's unforgiving. And Katie had a rebel streak in her that he tried to squelch six ways to Sunday."

"But—"

"No buts." Maude turned a firm gaze his way. "I've known that girl since she was in the cradle. And Howard's as responsible as any for her wild years.

He knows that, which is why he needs to blame you. Howard Bascomb isn't about to shoulder that responsibility himself."

"I was sixteen, driving the car and drunk." Matt laid out the facts with no defensive strategy. "I'm going with my fault."

"Huh." She sighed and looked aggrieved. "You're such a leatherneck."

Her use of the marine term made him smile. "Guilty."

"And two tours in Iraq."

"Didn't give Katie her leg back." He reached for the door handle, then turned back toward Maude. "I appreciate what you're trying to do."

"But you're too dad-gum stubborn to see it yourself," she shot back. "And that's the one thing you are guilty of, Matt Cavanaugh." She reached out a hand to shake his, her grip firm and direct. "I married a marine. Smartest move I ever made, so forgive an old lady for doing some matchmaking as opportunity arises."

"Yes, ma'am." He grinned, tipped his chin down and headed back into the rain, the bustle of people gone, the park round empty. He realized he'd half hoped Callie would still be here, which was downright silly because he'd see her back at the house in just a few minutes, right?

"Hey, marine."

He turned as her car rolled up alongside him, unable to fight back the smile of welcome. "Hey, yourself. You folks going the wrong way?"

Callie shook her head. "Just wanted to make sure everything was okay. I saw your truck parked here once I dragged Jake away from his buddies and..." She shrugged, pretending unconcern. "I didn't want you stuck or anything."

Add compassionate to her growing list of attributes, as if Matt needed more reasons to be attracted. He bent down, leaned in and grinned, pleased that she checked on him, staunchly refusing to examine why such a little thing felt so good.

Why did his smile make her heart feel stronger? Prettier? More desireable? Why did mere seconds in his company make her long for more?

You don't get it? Really?

Callie hushed the inner admonition. She *couldn't* get it, plain and simple. And since Matt understood the rules, they should do fine, right? "Then I'll see you at home and we can get started on the next group of windows, right?"

"Meaning you'll make food in the nice warm house while the rest of us install windows."

"And don't forget—" Jake began, excitement coloring his words.

"Christmas lights." Matt interrupted Jake with a grin and a wink. "And there's a great four o'clock game today." He gave his watch a pointed look.

"Reason enough for living right there," Callie drawled. "See you at home."

Her innocent phrase sparked something in Matt's eyes, a hint of longing that gave him a lost puppy look. The cool, crisp marine facade took over quickly, but Callie knew what she'd seen.

While not all soldiers bore physical wounds, all soldiers bore effects of service, good and bad. Life extracted nothing else.

But behind the wide smile, the patient hands, the warm embracing gaze, Matt's expression sought something. Yearning. Searching. Much like the face she saw in the mirror when no one was looking.

Pulling away, she refused to look back. Couldn't look back. Jake helped her out by pointing to the large sign at the front of the green. "Do you know how expensive those sleigh rides are, Mom?"

Callie shook her head.

"Way too pricey," Jake told her firmly. "And why would anybody need to go see Christmas lights when we can put up our own?"

Callie recognized the tactic and loved him for it. "You're right, of course. And we always take a drive to the neighborhoods and check out the lights, right?"

"For free."

A part of her wished that lack of money didn't govern every turn. Another part respected how Jake cared enough to accept certain things without haggle. "Free's a good thing these days. For a lot of people."

"And Shadow Jesus?"

She grinned, his innocence wiping away old thoughts of bad times. "After the lights. If not today, then one day this week after school."

"Good." They drove another minute forward before Jake twisted. A quick glance his way showed his concern. "Who was that guy yelling at Matt?"

Callie sighed. She'd hoped he'd missed that little confrontation on their first pass through town, but the kid was too smart for his own good. "That was Mr. Bascomb. I don't think he was yelling, honey. They were just talking."

Jake snorted. "He was mad, Mom. At Matt."

Conceding, she met him halfway. "He did look irritated."

"Ticked off." Jake shook his head. "I don't know why anybody would get mad at Matt. He's the best."

"He is." It wasn't bad to admit that, was it? Here in the privacy of their car, just her and Jake? "And if you want to help today, I'll have you work on window shims with us. The guys are coming by for a few hours to see if we can finish up."

"Cool." Jake swung open his door and turned Callie's way as they hurried toward the house. "And you don't have to pay me, Mom."

"Jake, people work to get paid. It's the norm. Blame our capitalistic society."

He grinned, held the door for her, then shrugged out of his jacket once they were on the porch. "I don't need money. You and Grandpa do. Really." He gazed up at her with earnest eyes, his expression firm. "I don't want you to pay me. I just want to help you and Grandpa."

Tears pricked her eyes.

"Aw, geez."

"You're such a good boy."

"Mom, get over it already." He ducked his head, shrugged under her arm and through the kitchen door, but sent her a teasing look over his shoulder, a look that reminded her of how Matt joked with her. Laughed with her.

"I'm getting changed for work."

Callie pegged her coat and headed upstairs behind him. "Me, too. And it looks like Grandpa's beat us over there with Buck and Jim, so we can get a quick start."

"I'm here, too." Tom's voice hailed her from down the stairs. "I'll meet you guys across the way. There's doughnuts on the table."

"Doughnuts! Thanks, Tom!"

Callie smiled, warmth seeking into her bones despite the cold rain.

Two weeks ago the future looked dim, Cobbled Creek looming like a dark abyss of failure.

Now?

She woke up excited each morning. To crew alongside the guys, watching these homes go together step by step... The entire process brightened her day, lightened her step.

She loved building. Creating. Operating power tools. Eyeing a square and a level, getting things just right. And not one of these men made her feel less feminine for her aptitude with a power hammer. So why had Dustin's rejection stung that much? That deep? Had she even loved him, or was their spontaneous marriage just a young lark gone bad?

She pulled on snug clothes, attached her tool belt

to the air-channeled suspenders and headed across the street with Jake, humming a tune, then realized she was humming the tune Matt whistled all the time.

His truck pulled up alongside them. "I thought you were cooking today? Staying warm?"

His gruff tone revealed more than the cautionary words. She tapped her watch and continued toward the subdivision. "I've got two hours before I have to start the chili and the bread. I can do a lot in two hours, marine."

She didn't wait to hear his response, but knew she'd pleased him and refused to question herself on why that felt particularly good.

"See ya over there, Matt!"

"I'll be right behind you, bud."

Callie wasn't sure what jack-hammered her heart out of its easy rhythm—his voice or choice of words. But the smile on Jake's face showcased Matt's dual effect.

And when he's gone, her conscience niggled. *What then?*

Callie shoved that aside. Homes weren't constructed overnight, and if Phase One of Cobbled Creek sold in quick fashion, Matt might expand his efforts into Phase Two, a second grouping of homes moving up the slope. In the meantime she intended to enjoy doing what she loved most. Working side by side with family and friends, making dreams come true.

Chapter Eight

"I've got this covered," Matt called down to Callie from the upper reaches of Hank's ladder late that afternoon, raising his voice above the rain. "It's not rocket science."

"Goes faster with two, especially in these conditions." Callie thumped the second ladder up against the house with military ease.

"Then send Buck out," Matt chastised, striving for patience. Wasn't this the day he wanted her to rest up? Stay warm and dry? She'd been working or cooking since they got home from church. Not exactly the R & R he'd envisioned.

"I would, but he's sound asleep in the recliner." She adjusted her ladder, drove in a couple of quick stakes to maintain the position and headed up the rungs, Christmas lights suspended from her shoulders.

"Nice necklace."

The rain blocked her grin, but he pictured her wide smile. Her reply only deepened the vision. "I wore it for you."

"And the boots?"

She laughed, and the bright sound eased the steady torment of being perpetually wet for nearly seventy-two hours. "Bloomingdale's. Like 'em?"

She waggled her foot off the edge of the ladder and he had a sudden urge to save and scold.

He quelled both. "Bloomingdale's carries army surplus? Sweet."

She began unwinding the lights from her neck, slipping the cord through the permanently affixed light hangers along the roofline, the long extension cord flagging in the wind and rain.

Matt worked her way until he had to shift his ladder. He climbed down, made his adjustment, then realized how close they were to being done as he headed back up. "I didn't realize this would go so fast."

"Dad put in the hangers years ago. And it takes exactly two strings minus eight inches, so when I get to the middle, we should meet up and be perfect."

Matt knew he should resist, but an opening like that was made to be used. "Nothing I haven't been saying right along, Cal."

"Ha, ha." She reached out, hooked a light, scrambled down the ladder way too quickly for his peace of mind and the wet conditions, moved it three feet toward center, applied her stakes and headed back up.

"You're quick," he observed, noting how much closer she was now. Touchable, actually.

"What I am is soaked," she shot back, deftly stringing the green wire through the last of the turned brackets. "And cold. Hence the speed."

"I'd feel sorry for you if you hadn't totally ignored instructions." Matt reached left as she finished the length of her light string and grabbed her hand as well as the cord. "I could have done this. I was already wet. And I wanted you to have one day to be comfortable. Warm. Dry."

"Well." She slanted him a smiling look, then swept their linked hands a glance. "This way I got you to hold my hand."

"Honey, you didn't need to climb a ladder in the rain for that. I'd have obliged under much more hospitable conditions."

She winked, wiggled her hand free, then watched him connect the two ends. "Someday when you're not my boss, we'll talk."

"Back to that." He climbed down the ladder as she did, stepped off and reached out, tugging her closer, her look of surprise and wonder saying more than words ever could. He held her gaze and her hand, the rain soaking through their hats, their neck warmers, their hoodies. "I can't even fire you for my own selfish purposes because you're too good at what you do, Callie."

A smile stole across her face, a look of pleasure that hinted more than humor. "Thank you for saying that."

He grinned, dropped her hand but wished he didn't have to, removed his ladder stakes and hers, then shooed her toward the house in a no-nonsense voice.

"I only speak the truth, ma'am. Go inside. Sit by the fire. Get warm. I'll put the ladders away."

She looked about to argue, but then that hinted contentment invaded her features again, as if having someone watch over her was the most magnificent thing in the world. And that only made Matt want to do it more.

Except he couldn't. At least not right now.

Not ever, soldier. You think she'd be all doe-eyed and sweet-talkin' when she hears how you passed your teen years? Detoxing in a detention center after wrecking people's lives?

And yet, Katie hadn't looked wrecked that morning. She'd looked…wonderful. Content. Peaceful. And her spark of humor that earned them more than one scolding in junior high was evident in the grin she flashed the congregation as she challenged them with her fiddle.

What had Staff Sergeant Weckford told him years ago? "Never let a memory become stronger than a dream."

Matt thought he understood the inference, but relocating to Jamison and Wellsville, seeing old haunts, old friends, new faces… His head accepted the practicality of moving on.

His heart longed for a do-over.

"Fire's nice and toasty," Hank greeted him as he came in. The warmth enveloped Matt, a comfort that came from more than the wood stove fire, although he wouldn't deny the welcome the DutchWest offered.

There was Jake, sprawled in front of the game, a bowl of popcorn to the side, maneuvering a team of soldiers through dense jungles of Pacific islands. Buck, head back, sound asleep in Hank's recliner, looking utterly content. And as Hank grabbed Matt's soaked hoodie and hung it near the fire to dry, Callie hustled down the stairs, a pair of fitted jeans replacing her loose working variety, while an aqua knit turtleneck hugged her like a second skin, the ribbed knit looking comfy-cozy while it showcased curves her work gear camouflaged.

If Matt had a hard time getting her off his mind in flannels and hoodies, he'd jump straight to impossible now, the soft blue-green knit complementing her green eyes.

She looked absolutely beautiful and if Hank hadn't clapped him on the back as the home team scored on their opening drive, he probably would have stood and stared for who knows how long. Forever, maybe?

His family didn't do forever, not since Grandpa's time, but seeing Callie here, in the worn but genteel home setting, Matt began to realize that no one charted his destiny but him. Sure, he had a past.

Who didn't?

But maybe, just maybe, he'd be able to have a future, too. At that moment it seemed almost doable.

Jake spotted him and jumped up, a welcome interruption. "Are the lights hooked up?"

Appreciation for the boy's eagerness turned his serious thoughts to more youthful pastimes. "Yes.

Once it gets dark, all you have to do is plug them in, bud."

"And it's getting dark earlier and earlier," Jake noted.

"Ah, to be the age when that was a joyous thing," Callie muttered to Matt. "And then tomorrow we'll put up the Holy Family."

"Not tonight?" A hint of whining drew Callie's gaze around.

"No. And no arguing. Everybody's been working hard all week. Tonight is rest time."

"Although I might be talked into a reenactment of our Aussie mates holding off a blitzkrieg on the carpet," Matt told him. "Once I get cleaned up."

Jake's brows shot up. "Really?"

"Jacob Henry."

Jake shot a quick glance to his mother. "If you're too tired, Matt, it's okay."

"Let me take care of this wet stuff." Matt made a face that had both Callie and Hank nodding agreement. "And then some of your mother's amazing chili."

"And her fresh bread," shot in Buck, awake just in time to publicly laud Callie's achievements.

"And that, of course." Matt let his eyes twinkle into Callie's, his thoughts only partially on food. "And then I'm yours, bud."

Callie moved closer, but kept her voice low. "You wanted to watch the game. It's okay to tell him 'no.' He'll survive. Promise."

Matt matched his voice to hers. "My way means I

score points with the kid *and* his mother while Rodgers puts the offense over the top. Everybody wins."

The hint of color inspired by his banter made him long to touch her cheek. Feel the heat there. Maybe steal a kiss.

But a gentleman didn't toy with a lady's affections, especially a lady who'd been raked over the coals by someone not smart enough to realize how wonderful she was.

Exactly why he *couldn't* step out and act on his feelings. She didn't need more hurt or heartache, he was pretty sure of that. What she did need was money to cover basic things like food and shelter. One mess-up wouldn't only cost him great laborers, but it would also cost her the simple basics of life. Home. Heat. Groceries.

He'd cling to common sense. Help out quietly because he was living there. And try to think of a way to keep his distance, but seeing Callie in her everyday, nonconstruction clothes?

That image added a whole new level of difficulty to his task.

He noticed.
He noticed not.
He noticed...
Callie bit back a growl the next day, seriously disgruntled with herself, men in general, Matt in particular.

A convent would be so much easier.

"Callie, your level's off."

She jerked straight and eyed her bubble, chagrined. "Sorry, boss."

"No big deal. You feeling all right?"

Ignore the concern in his voice and the look on his face that says you matter. Trust me, you don't, except as a means to an end which is getting these roofs in place now that the rain has passed. "Fine. Just thinking."

"Stop that, okay?"

Eyes down, she nodded, knowing he was joking but unable to reciprocate. "Won't happen again."

He stopped nailing and whistling, the sudden silence making them seem like the only two people on Earth, but that was silly because her father, Jim and Buck were on the opposite side of the street installing underlayment over the plywood roofing on the last house.

"Hey." He moved closer and bent low. "You okay, Cal?"

"Yes, thanks for asking."

He didn't tease her back, didn't chuck her on the shoulder, didn't take the bait. "You sure?"

"Quite. And busy. How 'bout you?"

He touched a hand to her shoulder, a simple gesture of friendship, so why did it feel as if he was ready to lay down his jacket over the puddles in her life?

Too many puddles, not enough Carhartt.

Finch McGee's van pulled in, followed by Amanda Slaughter. Matt paused at the ladder and caught her eye. "It's almost worth not having coffee to avoid him."

"Tell me something I don't know." She waited one beat, then two, eyeing the ladder. "Are you waiting for me to go first?"

Matt shook his head, his gaze thoughtful, then inclined his gaze toward Finch's truck. "Does he ever bother you, Cal? I mean, *really* bother you?"

She hid the part of her that longed to bask in his concern because Callie knew what Matt meant by "bother." "Matt, I might have been army to your marine credentials, but I can usually take care of myself. I am trained in mortal combat, remember?"

"And I'd welcome a personal demonstration sometime," he quipped back, but the hand to her shoulder returned. "If anyone ever pesters you, I've got your back, okay?"

"It's not like they're lining up on the street, marine." She stepped onto the ladder in front of him and shot him a disbelieving look.

"A situation I haven't been able to figure out," he told her as he climbed down after her. "Guys down here aren't the sharpest tools in the shed."

"And here's a rope to prove it," Callie muttered as Finch approached. She beelined for the coffee, successfully side-stepping Finch, leaving Matt to deal with him.

Cowardly?

No.

Self-preservation at its finest. For some reason Finch McGee had set his sights on Callie either because she was in financial constraints and possibly an easy target, or he wanted to make a full one-eighty away from his blonde, petite ex-wife.

Either way, she wasn't interested, but he wasn't an easily discouraged guy.

She loved that about Matt.

It annoyed her with Finch.

"Things are really coming along." Amanda noted as she handed Callie an insulated cup. "You guys have done a great job and Jim said he's never worked with a better crew."

"Back at ya." Callie raised her cup, sniffed and smiled. "I love that you buy me girly coffee with flavored creamers. That makes my day. You know that, right?"

Amanda leaned alongside the truck and watched as Jim joined Matt and the building inspector. "We girls have to stick together. And protect our men from snakes in the grass."

Callie didn't have to follow her look to know it embraced McGee. "Except I don't have a man, so we'll join forces to protect yours."

Eyes forward, Amanda sipped her coffee and grinned. "You keep telling yourself that, honey. According to my husband, aka Mr. Obtuse, Matt Cavanaugh can't keep his eyes off you."

Callie stretched out her flannel covered arm. Worn, faded flannel at that. She swept her working attire a disparaging look. "Are ya kiddin' me?"

"Good men see beyond what we wear."

Callie made a face. "That sounds so wrong."

Amanda laughed. "It did, kind of, but you know what I mean. They see our heart. Our soul."

"You're watching that *Tender November* romance series on PBS, aren't you?"

Amanda didn't confess, but she did sigh. "Brontës. Austen. Alcott."

"No wonder you're twitterpated." Callie dipped her chin as the men headed their way. "Let's ix-nay the omance-ray, okay?"

"If you insist."

"Oh, I do." Callie straightened as Matt reached across for the coffee bearing his initials.

"Thanks, Amanda."

"You're welcome. Finch, I'm sorry, I'd have grabbed you a coffee if I'd known you were going to be here."

"Just had one, thanks." Finch's expression and tone eased up as he answered Amanda, then hardened again as he indicated his reason for stopping by. The one that *didn't* include checking out Callie. "I wanted to make sure those berms were re-covered with tarp and straw. Topsoil doesn't grow on trees."

"No, it doesn't," Amanda agreed.

Amanda's straight face only strengthened Callie's urge to laugh. Jake's school bus rumbled down the road, its caution lights flashing, a perfect diversion. "I'll be right back," she said to Matt with a wave toward Jake. "And I'll bring Jake over for cleanup."

She wasn't quite quick enough because Finch managed to fall into step beside her as she headed for the road. Figuring she'd lose him at his truck, a shot of dismay hit her when he didn't open the door and get in. No, he stayed alongside her, giving him ample opportunity to talk when the last thing she wanted to do was listen.

"I miss seeing you at the diner."

Face first, eyes forward. "I love what I'm doing here, though. If this could last forever, I'd be a happy girl."

"Lots of ways to find happiness, Callie."

Just when she thought she'd have to turn around and slug him in the solar plexus, Matt appeared alongside them. "Those notes for number seventeen are still on Hank's desk, right?"

Thank you, God. And thank you, Matt. "They are, yes. Would you like me to get them?" *Please say no. Please say you'll get them yourself and walk me to the house.*

"I'll grab them. I'm going to have the plumbing and electricity inspected before we apply the drywall, and I want to familiarize myself with the layout changes your dad made."

"Like the built-in bookshelves in each bedroom?"

"Exactly that. So, Mr. McGee? Is Wednesday good for you?"

Matt stopped along the road, his presence an obvious wrench in the other man's works.

Finch stopped, faltered, then nodded. "And you know I'm a stickler for code, right, Cavanaugh?"

The way Finch used Matt's last name, coupled with his caustic tone, made Callie want to give him a good, swift kick.

But nothing got inhabited without Finch's signature. Ticking off the building inspector who was also a zoning agent wouldn't be in anyone's best interest. He'd already shown disrespect for Matt, and that tweaked Callie's protective instincts because Finch had no cause. The people who moved into these sweet homes wouldn't have to worry that the builder cut corners. So why was Finch nailing Matt with a glare? Because of her?

Ridiculous.

"And I appreciate that, Mr. McGee." Matt kept his tone level, but there was no mistaking granite for anything else. He'd be polite because they were professionals, but his voice and stance said he didn't back down. Ever.

Finch drew a hint closer, just a smidge, as if trying to intimidate Matt. Not much intimidated a marine. Callie loved that.

"Mom!"

"Go get changed, Jake." Callie called across the two-lane road. "We're coming."

"Wednesday, Cavanaugh."

Matt nodded as if Finch weren't acting like a first-class bully, then headed toward the street with Callie.

"He was a jerk to you."

Matt glanced both ways before heading across. "Who cares?"

"I do."

"Aw." He slowed his step and shoulder-nudged her, an easy grin erasing the whispered pain she'd seen with Finch's tone. His words. But nothing bothered Matt, right?

"I knew you cared, Cal. Thanks for admitting it."

"I care about seeing a friend get rudely dismissed by a guy who shouldn't be washing your bootstraps."

"As I have done for others, so you should do." Matt settled a gentle look on her. "Christ washed the apostles' feet and told them to humble themselves. Humility isn't a bad thing."

"I don't think he was talking about Finch McGee."

Matt caught her arm just outside the door. "Sure he was. To a point." He shifted his gaze to Cobbled Creek Lane where Finch waited for a car to pass before heading back toward Jamison. "His words can't hurt me, Callie. His actions can. And in the interest of time and funding, I'll let his rudeness slide. If we get this section done and sold and go on to Phase Two of the subdivision, then I'll ask to have Colby Dennis oversee our work."

He said "our work" like it was a given. Callie choked back a surge of anticipation because nothing was a given these days in home-building. Matt had taken a big risk by buying Cobbled Creek. She prayed daily that all would go well, although that hadn't come close to working in her father's case.

Oh, honey, I think the answer to your prayers is about eight inches from you, front and center.

Callie hushed her inner voice, but not before heat climbed to her face as they headed inside.

"You blushing, Cal?"

"Exertion."

A knowing grin set the laugh lines around Matt's gorgeous brown eyes a little deeper. "Coffee drinking is hard work." He took in her cup and her heated cheeks with a swift look of amusement. "So." He glanced around, the sound of Jake getting ready punctuated by things hitting the floor above them. "What did you come over here for?"

"To avoid Finch."

He burst out laughing and grabbed her in a hug, a spontaneous and wonderful two-arms-wrapped-around-you kind of hug that couldn't have been more perfect if he'd tried.

Until his laughter paused. His arms tightened, the grip different. Wonderfully different.

Should she look up at him?

Yes.

No.

But she did because there was no way she *couldn't* look up. Gaze into those coffee-no-cream eyes. See the look of gentle awareness there, the strength of a good man, a man who talked of washing feet and building homes, a man who walked with God and fellow soldiers.

"Callie…"

He whispered her name about the same time he feathered a kiss across her lips, the feel of strong, gentle and muscled arms tumbling her into a world of possibilities she hadn't dreamed feasible in a long time.

"Mom! Do you know where my thick socks are?"

Callie stepped back, joy and chagrin vying for emotional space. "Try the laundry basket in the hall."

"Got 'em!"

"Good."

"Very good." Matt whispered agreement and stroked one finger across the intensified heat in her cheeks. "I'd apologize, ma'am, but I'm not a bit sorry."

"No?"

"Oh, no." He stepped back as Jake's racing footfall announced his eager approach. "I had to know."

Know?

Oh, man.

"Ready, guys. I've got my stuff." Jake patted his waist where a smaller version of their belts held a boy-sized set of tools, his hard hat clutched tight in the other hand.

"You know you're on cleanup, right?" Callie sent his tool belt a hiked-brow look. "You probably won't need those today."

Jake's face fell. His lower lip hinted a quiver. "At all?"

"Not today, bud, but how about you work with me on Thanksgiving while Mom cooks?"

"Who said I'm cooking?" Callie drew herself up to her full height and met Matt's gaze straight on. "Why is it the girl gets elected to cook while the guys play with power tools?"

Matt's look of surprise said she got him. "I just thought—"

"You thought wrong." Callie waved a hand toward the kitchen behind them and figured they might as well get this straight. "I cook because I have to.

I build because I can't *not* build. There's a difference, Matt."

"There is." He contemplated her, made a face and ran a hand across the back of his head. "But it *is* Thanksgiving, so someone has to cook, right? Maybe we can break it down? Do different jobs?"

She smiled, nodded and whacked his arm. "Now you're talkin', marine. And if we order pies from the bakery, that's one more thing I don't have to do."

Matt wasn't about to say that the very thought of homemade pies brought him to his knees. It had been a lot of years since he'd shared a holiday meal with anyone, so the anticipation of joining hands for Thanksgiving around the Marek table had painted a slightly different picture in his head.

Obviously the wrong one. Therefore… "I'm picking up the turkey tomorrow." He followed Callie and Jake out the door and down the porch stairs, The General loping alongside them, his shaggy ears keeping time. "We can pick up the pies Thursday morning."

"And make stuffing and sweet potatoes Wednesday night."

Now things were looking up. "Squash?"

Callie made a face.

"Okay, no squash. Jello?"

"I love Jello!" Jake fist-pumped that idea.

"One yes takes the prize on that one. Rolls?"

"Same bakery we get the pies from."

"Gravy?"

"Dad makes the best gravy known to humankind."

Matt ran the list through his head and nodded, surprised. "So we can actually all work on Thursday morning."

"Now you're getting it." Callie grinned up at him, her friendly smile ignoring the sweet kiss they'd just shared while his heart was counting the possible moments until they might share kiss number two.

His phone rang. McGee's number flashed in the display box, reminding Matt of why he couldn't pursue this delightful road with Callie while he let the call go to voice mail. Reason number one jogged ahead of them, the dog keeping pace.

Callie thought she knew him. She knew the improved version. No way would a strong, forthright woman like Callie want the old version around her kid. Her home. Her life.

Hank knew. Matt understood that.

But Callie didn't have a clue. That was evident in her easy manner. The calm, admiring looks she'd shift his way as the houses began to come together.

No doubt Hank was waiting for Matt to tell her. And he'd do that soon. Better to have this out in the open than let worry fritter away his heart, his soul. He had enough of that after seeing Katie, knowing he had to face her, another confrontation he needed to schedule.

Once the roofs were on and the windows in, he'd face his past with both women. Not wanting to do a job didn't get a man out of that job. Not a marine, anyway.

The houses should be sealed by the first Sunday

of Advent. Then he'd switch gears and concentrate on completing the model, starting with the kitchen cabinets he hoped to put in on Thursday and Friday when they'd be low on help. By Saturday, Jim would be back to work, and Tom, too.

"Lost you, marine."

He sent her a quick look of apology. "Planning. Strategizing."

She nodded, having no clue that his plans might very well disrupt their working relationship. Once Callie realized the guy flirting with her had been a teenaged con, a whole lot of things would most likely change. The thoughts of that kiss, of seeking a different bond that went beyond work?

That would probably tank as well, but he'd be unfair to take this further without Callie's awareness, and Matt had vowed to never be unfair again.

Chapter Nine

"This is the coolest thing I've ever seen, bud." Matt finished positioning stakes meant to tether the wood-sculpted Holy Family into place on Wednesday night, then motioned Jake left. "Shall we turn on the spotlights, see what we've got?"

"Just make sure they're centered, or Mom will move 'em."

"Got it. See if anybody else wants to watch the lighting ceremony."

Jake dashed up the porch steps, calling for Hank and Callie while Matt stepped back, eyeing left, then right.

Centered.

Then he examined the spotlight positions, knowing that could slant the image.

Also centered.

He smiled. Callie liked things focused. Symmetrical.

So did he.

She loved building. Climbing ladders. Working rooftops.

Ditto.

As Callie and Hank crossed the yard with Jake, Matt wondered what it would be like to be part of this family, a plan he'd never allowed himself. But at this moment, with these people, the vision seemed attainable.

Because you're living a lie.

Seeing Jake's grin and Callie's smile, he wouldn't think about that. Hank clapped him on the back as Jake flipped the switch, the colorful roofline lights adding nighttime wonder to the simply shadowed nativity scene below.

Matt's heart clenched, the reality of Bethlehem rubbing raw. They'd hobbled into town to find no room. No shelter, other than a cavelike barn. And a manger lined with coarse straw on a cold, winter's night. Little Jesus had been born there, in crude, meager conditions. Truly a child of the poor.

Like him.

"Hey." Callie moved alongside him, looking up as if he were the most wonderful thing in the world, all because he'd taken time to set up Jake's favorite Christmas decoration. "It's perfect."

"Centered properly?"

She laughed and hugged his arm. "Yes. Jake ratted me out, huh?"

"Nothing wrong with wanting things done correctly," Matt supposed. "And it saves a lot of work to do it right the first time."

Gazing forward, Hank's easy tone pondered Matt's pragmatic words. "But if we *do* mess up, God usually gives us chances to make amends. Embrace new ways."

His words targeted Matt. They both knew it. Matt breathed deep and shrugged, the thought of a baby born in less-than-perfect circumstances hitting home. One big difference pierced his heart like a three-penny nail. Christ lived his life sacrificially; Matt had messed up repeatedly. "Not everything's fixable, Hank."

"True enough," Hank replied. "But I try to never second guess God's vantage point. Ours is limited. Omniscience gives God the advantage to see all. Heal all."

How Matt wished that were true. But he'd seen the horror on Katie's face, the shock, the realization that she was damaged beyond repair. A look he put there through careless, callous misdeeds.

"Thanks, Matt!" Jake launched himself at Matt, hugging him, his excitement over the decorations innocent and contagious. Matt could do nothing less than haul the boy into his arms, wondering again what kind of moron ignored a great kid like Jake.

"You're welcome, bud. Hey, it's getting cold out here. Shall we head inside? Start those sweet potatoes?"

"Got 'em done while you boys were doing this," Hank announced as they moved toward the steps. "The cookin' part anyway. I'll do the glaze in the morning, then all we have to do is heat 'em up to go with the turkey."

"And I cut up all the bread for the stuffing," Jake

added as they pegged their jackets inside the door. "While Mom did the onions and celery."

"Teamwork." The idea of a family working together to produce a holiday meal was both alien and fun. Mostly fun. "Do I smell…?" Matt followed his nose toward the kitchen, then turned to see Callie watching him, waiting for his reaction. "You made pies?"

"I did. Not because I had to, mind you." She sent him a warning look and wagged her finger like The General wagged his ears. "Because I *wanted* to after you looked like a lost little boy when I said we'd buy them."

He pretended to scowl. "You weren't supposed to see that."

"Army training. And great peripheral vision. Anyway, what do you think?"

At that moment he thought she was the most remarkable, wonderful creature on Earth, but he couldn't say that out loud for a host of reasons. He cleared his throat and grabbed a fork from the table. "There's only one way to know for sure."

"Which will wait until tomorrow," she scolded, grabbing the fork. "But they smell great."

"Perfect."

She turned and met his smile, but the look on her face said she realized he was talking about more than the pies.

"Thanks, Callie."

"Well, you gave me plenty of time between the nativity scene and your book work."

"I hate keeping books," he admitted as he tugged off his shoes and set them by the fire. "And it's not even hard math, it's just tedious."

"Callie kept my books for me." Hank brought a plate of ham-melt sandwiches to the table, the quick supper a salute to Thursday's feast prep time. "And I can't say she didn't warn me we were skating thin ice a number of times."

"Everybody takes chances, Hank." Matt met his gaze candidly. "There are no givens. If you'd gotten this done before the housing bubble burst, you'd have been called a hero. But getting sick on top of rough financial circumstances." Matt shook his head. "Tough all around." He sat next to Jake, his attention on Callie. "But I'd be glad to pay you to take over my bookkeeping. Not much, of course," he added with a grin. "Are you familiar with QuickBooks?"

"I used it for Dad's records." She brought the coffee pot to the table and filled Hank's cup and his before topping off her own. "Which meant the bank could see there was no wrongdoing when things went bad. Just horrible timing."

"And overextending." Hank grimaced, then sighed. "But I've got to say, Matt, that having you here, working with you, seeing those houses take shape at last." Hank nodded his relief. "My dream is coming true, thanks to you."

"Thanks to us," Matt corrected smoothly. "And I've never worked with a better crew, including you, bud." He chucked Jake in the upper arm, making the boy grin. "So things worked out all around."

"And tomorrow…" Jake waved toward the front window, his mouth full, not waiting to swallow before reminding Matt of his promise.

Matt angled him a patient look. "Let's say grace. And yes, I remember. We're putting the kitchen in the model tomorrow and you're helping."

"Me, too," piped in Callie.

"Count me in," added Hank.

Matt waited as they joined hands, then lobbed a look around the table. "The whole family's rushing to get this kitchen done and the C of O signed?" He winked toward Jake. "Must be wearing out my welcome around here."

Callie squeezed his hand, her touch inciting sparks against his skin. "Oh, you're not so hard to take, marine. Kind of nice, actually. And you'll only be across the street. Easy visiting."

"Until the model sells," he added.

Her face shadowed.

Hank did his customary quick grace, and Callie let go of Matt's hand once done, but he had pretty good peripheral vision, too.

Was that a glimpse of misgiving because she'd put her heart and soul into that model?

Or because he'd move to town once the model sold?

But like it or not, he needed to get a couple of these houses contracted. And holiday time was the worst for selling homes. Most people avoided the time-consuming task of directing a building project until after New Year's. Which meant if the model caught someone's eye, he'd have to sell it and finish another home to occupy until spring.

"Wait on the Lord. Be of good courage and he shall strengthen thine heart. Wait, I say, on the Lord." The Psalm's sage advice had been his mainstay for a long time.

Patience. Perseverance. Persistence. Matt embraced these qualities as a marine, then again as a contractor, but with Cobbled Creek, a part of him longed to fast forward toward completion and the reason for that unusual impatience sat four short feet away, explaining why she'd chosen Golden Wheat stained maple for the Cape Cod's kitchen.

They'd passed the initial inspection today. Within a week or two the model should be deemed ready for occupancy. He'd listed the homes with local Realtor Mary Kay Hammond, but they both knew the score. December was a dead month in real estate sales.

And he should be fine financially as long as they contracted two of the houses before spring, then doubled that by summer.

"I'll have the turkey ready to go in at ten." Callie looked up from the list she was making. "So if we eat at four or so, that works out well, right?"

Matt propped his elbows on the table and leaned forward. "We could always take the day off like normal people do."

Three sets of eyes rounded on him like he'd sprouted an extra head.

"Why would we do that?" Callie asked.

"Yeah, why?" Jake echoed.

"I can't think of a thing to be more thankful for than seeing those houses cared for," added Hank. "If you're worried we'd rather have a day off, then you're sitting at the wrong table, son."

Their earnest desire eased Matt's conscience. "I can't imagine sitting at a finer table, sir."

Hank grinned. "Well, I do make a mean ham melt."

"And the coffee couldn't be better." Matt raised his cup toward Callie.

She ignored his grin and went back to her list. "Turkey at ten, potatoes and sweet potato casserole at three, rolls go in once the gravy's started."

"That way we catch the late game on TV," Jake added.

"With pie."

"And the day just keeps getting better and better." Matt hoisted his mug in salute. "To teamwork. And a beautiful Thanksgiving."

The house phone rang, interrupting the toast. Hank stood, picked it up, sent a quick glance Matt's way, then headed toward the back of the kitchen, his voice low.

"Who was that, Grandpa?" Jake asked when Hank returned to the table.

"Don."

"Is he coming tomorrow?"

The boy's innocent words caused a momentary discomfort. "Not this year."

"But—"

"He's busy, Jake."

"He's going somewhere else for supper?"

Hank was obviously no good at lying. "Well…"

"Jake, he's—"

Sensing the truth, Matt cleared his throat. "Hey, guys, it's fine if he comes. You know that, don't you?"

Hank exchanged a quiet look with Callie. "We'll leave things the way they are for now, I think."

"No, really, I…"

Callie shook her head and sent a swift cautionary look toward Jake. "Don's got plans already and it's not like we're going to be sitting around all afternoon chitchatting, right?"

That made sense to Jake, but Matt felt like a first-class heel. "Listen, if…"

Hank interrupted him, obviously not wanting to say too much with little ears around. "Plenty of time for Don to stop by over the winter. He's staying in town this year, so it's not like it usually is, Jake."

"Oh." Jake nodded as if they were finally making sense. He turned Matt's way. "Don always has Thanksgiving dinner with us before he goes to Florida. He's known Grandpa a long time."

"He's staying here this year?" Matt directed the question to Hank, but Callie answered.

"Yes. He figured it was best all around. Going to Florida isn't cheap and there's no guarantee of work once you get there."

Did Matt sense a hint of something else in her words? He thought so, and the quiet look she exchanged with her father confirmed his gut instinct. And Don needed work. He'd mentioned that.

But Matt had plenty of help right now. More than enough. He pushed his chair back and stood, the perfect holiday now shaded with guilt.

His father needed help. Except he wasn't *really* his father. And he'd abandoned him long ago. And he had a drinking problem.

Matt didn't do drinking problems. He didn't do family. He didn't embrace the American dream that had emotionally thrashed him as a kid. Thinking of Don brought up thoughts of Neal Brennan and his mother's duplicity, the lies, the scandal, the family breakdown that left him pretty much on his own from age eight.

"When my father and mother forsake me, then the Lord shall take me up."

God had done that in the form of Grandpa Gus, but not before Matt realized that bad apples produce like fruit and the idea of love, marriage and sweet, dimpled babies should be someone else's dream.

His dream?

To love God, love his work and build beautiful, affordable homes that withstood the test of time.

And that's it? Home to an empty apartment every night? A cold stove?

Yes. Less risk for everyone.

Matt met Hank's troubled gaze. "I'm going to turn in early. Get a jump on tomorrow. If you hear me head over before dawn, don't feel like you have to rush. We've got all day."

"Sure, Matt!"

Jake's grin showed oblivion to the rising concern surrounding the table, and just as well. Little boys didn't need to be surrounded by old drama.

Whereas big boys didn't have much of a choice.

"Hey, bud, good job."

Callie and Hank exchanged a smile as Matt advised Jake the next afternoon, the boy's rapt attention the best kind of hero worship.

"Like this, Matt?"

"Exactly like that."

Matt let him read the level and Callie couldn't miss the delight in the boy's eye as he bent slightly. "Perfect."

"I couldn't have done better," Matt assured him. "And I'm real particular about installing cabinets. Finishing kitchens."

"Why?"

Callie suspected he slid a look her way, but pretended oblivion. "Kitchens make women happy. They like their kitchens just so, no matter how much they cook. Or don't cook, as the case may be."

Yup. Definitely targeting her. Such a guy thing to do. Teasing by innuendo. Kind of enchanting, actually.

"And a kitchen's called the heart of the home," Matt went on, abutting the next cabinet group to the first set they'd installed. "People are drawn to the kitchen. It brings back memories for lots of folks."

Matt snapped his tape shut, and waved a hand around. "Your mom did a great job planning this one."

"She did." Hank agreed as he and Callie finished the lower bank of cabinets on the inside wall. "Pantry space, work space, and she picked out appliances that weren't top end but would last."

"Top end being ridiculously expensive," Callie added. "Unless you're a Food Network chef or planning a humongous family, a nice four-burner stove with a convection oven does everything I need it to do."

"Because you don't live to cook," Matt teased from across the room.

"You're a quick study, marine." She slanted him a look of approval as she and Hank marked space for the upper cabinets. "Eating is essential. Cooking isn't. Hence the impressive frozen food sections in today's grocery stores. And a fresh apple." She held up her half-eaten one as an example and grinned. "Lunch on the run."

"Because I've found myself inundated with crew members who tend to elongate their lunch hours rather than shorten them, let me just say I appreciate the difference more than most. The Marek family is amazing."

"Can't disagree." Hank stood, checked his watch and headed for the door. "I'm going across the street to check on the turkey and start the other stuff. No, General, you stay here." He waved the dog back into the front room. "I'll get the potatoes peeled and the table set. Then you guys come on over in an hour or so."

Another hour gave them time to finish those upper cabinets while Jake applied rustic-styled hardware to the lower ones. Callie nodded, balancing with one foot on the ladder, the other on the untopped cabinet unit below to get the best angle for drilling. "Sounds like a plan. Thanks, Dad."

Hank sent her a fond grin. "You're welcome."

"Like this, Matt?" Jake held out a burnished handle and lined it up with the holes Matt had drilled in the honey-toned maple doors.

"Yes." Matt crouched alongside the boy, looking like a proud father. Strong. Determined. Gentle. Stoic. "Now start the first screw just enough to hold things in place, then do the same with the second…" Matt paused while Jake followed instructions, his face a study in concentration while Matt looked on, smiling.

"You've got it."

"I did." Jake sent a grin Matt's way and high-fived him. "You can help Mom now. I've got this."

Callie bit back a laugh.

Matt straightened, patted Jake's shoulder and turned her way, his quiet look saying what they didn't dare say out loud.

The kid was outrageously cute, but at eight years old the last thing a sturdy boy like Jake wanted to hear was "cute."

Strong, yes. Tough? Most assuredly.

But cute?

Not so much.

Matt adjusted the cabinet jack below the first upper cabinet while Callie read the level. "We're good."

He handed her the drill and she did her best to ignore his proximity as she installed the holding screws, but that worked for all of two seconds.

Oops. Serious trouble. *When all else fails adopt a code of silence or go to inane conversation.*

Option two. It *was* a holiday. Silence seemed rude.

"You like this color for the cabinetry?"

Matt swept the kitchen a quick look. "It's great."

"I kept it light because even with south-facing windows, winter nights are long."

Matt nodded, agreeable. Maybe too agreeable. Which meant she might not want to talk about long winter nights. Cozy fires. Deer browsing for food beneath snow-swept hillsides.

"And I did the wall board in here myself," she continued as she settled the last screw into place on cabinet one.

"Lovely," he replied, but it only took one look to see the grin that said he wasn't just thinking about plaster board.

Maybe silence *was* a better choice.

"I like that you allowed space for built-in wall shelves flanking the fireplace in the living room," he told her.

"Dad's idea." Callie angled the drill until she felt the screw bite into the stud. "He said Mom begged for more storage space. Cupboards. Closets. Shelves.

And of course, like the shoemaker's wife goes barefoot, she was still waiting for those extra cupboards when she died."

"Sorry." He sent her a look of sympathy that made her feel like what she said mattered. "When did she pass away?"

"I was ten." She made a face as she sidestepped to the next cabinet. "It was rough, but she was a great woman. And Dad loved her so much, the kind of love everyone wants to find, you know?"

"Reason enough to write fiction, I guess."

"Ooh. Cynical." She sent him an over-the-shoulder frown. "Nothing wrong with happily ever afters, is there?"

"If they existed, no."

"And on that note…" She sent him a "let's change the subject" look and quipped, "About the weather we're having lately…"

"Safe topic."

"Weather is what it is. Human relationships?" Callie flashed him a grin and shrugged. "Whole other box of tools."

The General stood, paced to the door and whined. "Jake, can you take The General out, please?"

"Okay."

Once Jake had pulled on his thick hoodie and dashed outside with the dog, Callie nudged Matt for his attention.

"Hmm?" He looked up, a pencil held tight in his teeth, his square positioned to mark the outside of the last wall cabinet on that side.

Callie jerked her head toward the door. "You did a great job working with him."

Matt shook it off. "No big deal."

Callie hesitated, then waded in. "It *was* a big deal to Jake. He loves learning the trade. Trying his hand at things. And when we were working steady two years ago, he was too small to be much help but he longed to learn." She settled a warm look on the work-in-progress kitchen. "This is what he's been waiting for. A chance to try his hand at things. Be the apprentice. I just wanted to say thank you when he wasn't around."

Her heartfelt words made Matt suck in a breath, and her sweet expression loosened a rusty internal clamp left over from his painful childhood. He glanced away, wondering how much to say, then shrugged, wondering where the shot of pain came from after all this time. He'd thought it erased, two decades of good negating one of bad.

Obviously it didn't work that way.

"My grandfather taught me a lot of what I know," he told her but didn't meet her gaze. "He was a lot like your dad. Strong. Kind. Straight-shooting. And he loved God, heart and soul."

"You miss him."

"Oh, yeah." Matt hauled in a breath, then swept the well-apportioned house a look of appreciation. 'But mostly I want him proud. I want him watching me from heaven, knowing I stayed on the straight and narrow. Knowing I didn't stray. That I listened to everything he said and carried it with me."

"He knows."

"You think?" Matt faced her, hands out.

Callie smiled down at him, her look endearing. Engaging. "Oh, yes. I believe that utterly. When I've messed up, I can almost feel my mother's arm around me, saying, 'Well, then. Fix it.'"

Matt smiled. "Exactly." He hesitated, then waded into last night's dinner dilemma. "You know that Don's my stepfather."

Callie nodded as she applied the next screw. "Dad said as much. But that's all he said. And I couldn't wrestle information out of Buck either, so that's all I know."

"Neal Brennan was my father."

Callie stopped working and turned full about. "Jeff's father?"

"And Meredith's. Yes."

"Meredith was a year ahead of me in school," Callie mused. "Beautiful. Polished. Cheerleader. I didn't know her, but a part of me would have loved to be just like her."

"Kids hide a lot under an illusion of success."

"Did you?"

He snorted. "Not hardly. I went the other way."

Her expression said "Tell me more," but he wasn't about to spill everything here and now, when Jake would rejoin them at any moment.

"So Don married your mother…"

"If only it was that easy." Matt finished leveling

the last cabinets, face forward. "My mother cheated on Don. She was a waitress, Neal was a customer. A rich customer. I was the result. No one knew until Neal made it public knowledge when I was eight years old. Don walked out, started drinking, and I never heard from him again. My mother began entertaining guy after guy, never happy. Never content. She died during my first tour in Iraq."

"Oh, Matt." Callie touched his arm, sympathetic. "I'm so sorry."

"Yeah, well." He shrugged one shoulder, and changed the subject, feeling like he'd shared enough darkness to shadow a blessed holiday. "We're good here."

Jake burst back through the door, scrubbing his hands together, the dog trotting alongside. "It got cold out there."

Matt knew that. And working in a house all day with no heat wasn't exactly comfortable, even with their layers. "One more cabinet and we'll call it a day. I've got to grab a few things at the lumber yard in the morning, so I'll head over first thing. They open at six."

"It's Black Friday," Callie reminded him.

He'd forgotten that.

"Most of the craziness will be at the big stores and the shopping areas in Olean, but…" she let her voice taper and shifted a brow up, "the lumber yard had an ad in today's paper, so they'll be busy."

He should have made the run yesterday, but he didn't and he hated standing in line.

"Shop-a-phobic?"

He grunted. "Not when there's a point to it. But Black Friday?"

"Want me to go instead?" she asked as she applied the last two mounting screws.

Matt shook his head as he and Jake gathered tools. "No. My bad. And if they have a quick lane open, I'll still be able to get in and out."

Callie's doubtful look said that wasn't going to happen, but Matt could hope, right?

"This is amazing, Hank." Matt walked into the dining area a short while later and swallowed a lumber-sized lump in his throat, the laden table set for four. "What can I do to help?"

Hank beamed. "Have a seat. We're all set except for mashing the potatoes and saying grace. Only thing is, Callie doesn't let me get away with quick grace on Thanksgiving, so I might hold off and do the potatoes after we pray."

"Funny, Dad."

Hank grinned her way, his pride and affection for Callie and Jake obvious, and as they finished drying their hands and settled in at the festive table, one of Matt's heart clamps loosened a little bit more.

He fit at this table. With this family.

He didn't dare make too much of that. He comprehended the darkness of past sins.

But it felt good to be here. Real good. And Matt hadn't sat at a family table to have a holiday dinner in fifteen years, so this…

Oh, this was nice.

They joined hands, heads bowed as Hank said the blessing, and while slightly longer than his usual, it wasn't overdone to the point of cold potatoes.

"You were right." Callie sent Matt a look of unsurpassed happiness a few minutes later. "This turkey is magnificent."

He grinned. "Told you so."

"Son, I haven't had a bird taste this good in a long time," Hank confessed. "We always buy the frozen ones they sell cheap in November. This—" he speared a piece of white meat and held it aloft "—reminds me of turkeys we had when I was a boy, when my parents would go to the farm and pick their out."

"Free range. Some mighty good eating right there."

"And even though I'm eating a feast," Callie confessed, "I'm already envisioning turkey sandwiches with cranberry sauce. Turkey and biscuits. Turkey and rice."

"And pie," Matt added with enthusiasm.

His tone of appreciation made her flush. "Now the pressure's on. What if they're not good?"

"They'll be wonderful."

"You used your mama's crust recipe, and crust makes the pie," Hank declared. "Now, Jake, if you'll hand me that dish of sweet potatoes, I think I've cleared a corner on this plate of mine."

Jake laughed and passed the bowl left, his eagerness for food warding off the urge to converse, unusual for Jake. But Matt understood the boy's attentiveness to a meal like this, and couldn't deny he felt the same way.

Warm. Fed. A place to belong.

Guilt niggled him out of nowhere.

Where was Don tonight? Did he catch Thanksgiving dinner with a friend? Or had this been his only option and Matt ruined it by being there?

Sizing up the amount of food they had, the twinge of guilt grew. There'd have been plenty of food for Don and leftovers.

Did he want his former stepfather hanging around? No.

But that gut feeling went against the grain of faith Matt knew better. And if his original reason to work in southern Allegheny County was to mend old fences, he could have started with Don.

"Matt, you okay?" Jake asked when he'd been quiet too long.

"I'm fine, bud. Just thinking of how wonderful this is. How blessed I am to be here."

Hank met his look across the table. Read his mind Matt saw it in a tiny flash of satisfaction that crinkled Hank's gaze.

He'd messed up by leaving Don out of this equation. But because Don was staying in town for the winter, Matt could find some way to fix it.

Add it to the list, his conscience scoffed. *And tha list is getting a little long, don't you think?*

It was, but Thanksgiving night was a time for rejoicing. Eating pie. Watching football and the firs Christmas specials.

"More stuffing, Matt?"

Callie offered the green-glazed bowl full of the most delicious stuffing he'd ever tasted, the bowl's color contrasting with the lighter green of her eyes.

"Yes, please. It's the best I've ever had, Callie."

Gladness brightened her features, but she angled him a warning look, sassy and spritely, total Callie. "Don't get used to it. I'd rather build, remember?"

"I won't likely forget. Nor would you let me."

But right then the thought of building together, eating together, grabbing frozen food together...

That seemed too good to be true, but for tonight, this night, he'd relax and enjoy the moment.

Chapter Ten

"Cavanaugh."

Matt cringed inside the next morning. Outwardly, he showed no emotion as Finch McGee sauntered his way, the lumber yard registers doing a brisk Black Friday business. "Mr. McGee. Did you have a nice Thanksgiving?"

McGee's glare contradicted his positive reply. "Fine." He scanned the box of hardware Matt held, the bite in his look unbecoming. "Not taking time off?"

"Time is money."

"It is." McGee drew closer. Too close. Matt resisted the urge to step back, the people behind him too close to allow room, and not wanting to give Finch the satisfaction of knowing he crowded him. But he also didn't want to pick a fight with the building inspector.

"And you know I'm watching you, right?"

Matt fought a sigh. McGee's attitude was growing tedious. And unless he missed his guess, the faint scent of hops meant Finch hadn't gone to bed sober last night. Great. "Any advice I get on finishing those homes is welcome."

"Oh, I'm not advising you." Finch leaned in closer, the rising volume of his voice drawing glances from nearby shoppers, strains of Christmas music blotted out by the building inspector's mounting tirade. "I'm hounding you. Watching. Waiting. Wondering when you're going to screw up again because I know you will. Your kind always does."

Should he set the hardware down and leave quietly, avoiding a scene?

The combined attention of the cashiers flanking them and the people in line said it was too late for that.

Change of subject?

One look at Finch's bloodshot eyes negated that option.

He'd punt the ball, figuratively. "Mr. McGee, what do you think of Councilman Gilroody's suggestion requiring all new housing to have metal roofs?"

McGee stepped back, confused.

Perfect.

"The one-time expense drives initial prices up," Matt continued as he moved closer to checking out and a much-needed escape, "but the home's value stays steady and gives banks less reason to refuse a mortgage, so the long-run offering is substantial."

"Gilroody's a good man."

Matt knew that. And the quick change of subject had gotten him to the cash register, so mission complete. "And the extended life warranty on those roofs is attractive."

Finch gathered his thoughts just long enough for the young woman to ring up Matt's purchases. He smiled at her, accepted the bag of hardware needed to finish off the kitchen in the Cape, then turned toward the door.

"Remember, Cavanaugh."

Matt headed out, saying nothing, unwilling to feed the other man's hungover angst.

Maybe Finch had a drinking problem. From the look of him, he shouldn't have been driving, and Matt could attest that he shouldn't have been talking either, his posture and words drawing attention from a crowd.

It was foolish behavior for a town official, but in Matt's experience, even a little power could turn a man's head. But Finch was in a position to cost Matt two things he couldn't afford to waste: money and time.

He needed Phase One complete before he requested Colby as his inspector. That good faith initiative went far in town government, and Matt was determined to make the grade, but Finch's attitude said this was far from over, and that didn't bode well.

He paused as he backed up the truck. He could return to Cobbled Creek and think about offering Don a job or he could man up and do it.

The clock told him it was early, but construction crews weren't much for sleeping in and Matt had looked up Don's address the night before. He had an apartment in Wellsville, five minutes from the lumber store.

Jesus had seized every opportunity to bring his lambs home. He'd gone hungry and thirsty to teach. He'd supped with sinners regularly, pressing the message that all were welcome at God's table.

Doing less felt wrong because it *was* wrong. Matt shoved the truck into drive and headed into Wellsville, hoping Don was awake. And sober.

"Matt?" Don scrubbed a hand to a lightly whiskered face and squinted at him in the doorway. "What are you doing here?"

"May I come in?"

"Sure." Don pushed the door open wider and let Matt into a threadbare apartment that smelled like coffee. "Want some coffee?"

"Please."

Don led him into the galley kitchen and filled two chipped mugs. "Got milk here."

"Black's fine."

"Sugar?"

Matt shook his head and figured they'd pretty much exhausted small talk. "You said you needed a job."

Don flushed, tentative. "I'm doing fine, actually. I've got some things lined up in Florida…"

"Except you're not going to Florida."

Don frowned. "Hank told you, huh?"

"Look, Don." Matt sat down in one of the two available chairs and pretended to be at ease. "I need a good drywall seamer. Hank says you're the best around."

"He's right."

"You've got to have steady hands to run seam."

"That's your way of saying no drinking." Don paused, glanced around, then met Matt's gaze. "I don't drink anymore, although there are days I want to. And the more I sit around, the harder that seems, but I don't want a job out of pity." He shifted forward, his gaze intent. "I did you wrong, Matt. I got mad at your mother for living a lie and I walked out, thinking biology made a man a father."

Matt gripped his coffee cup, unwilling to interrupt.

"I tossed eight years of loving you, being your dad, being so proud I could bust, into the trash over a cheating woman. It was a shameful thing to do. Between your mother and me, we did a lousy number on you and you ended up hanging with the wrong crowd, getting into all kinds of trouble. Considering that," Don hunched forward, his eyes clear, his expression guarded, "why would you offer me a job?"

"Because it's the right thing to do." Matt leaned forward as well, but not as far.

Regret shadowed Don's his features.

"I messed up big time," Matt continued. "But that was my fault as much as anybody's. I didn't hang with the wrong crowd, Don. I *was* the wrong crowd." He took one last long swig of coffee and stood. "I'm not good at all this talking stuff."

"Me neither."

"I need a seamer. I'd like us to get along. I can't have drinking around me, but if you're comfortable with that, I'd like to have you on board while the others work on sealing the remaining houses before the weather gets worse."

"Snow's forecast for next week."

"Which gives me just enough time if all goes well."

Don stretched out a hand, not a tremor in sight. "I'm in. And thank you, Matt."

A simple handshake between two construction guys. Why did it feel like so much more? "Head over once you're ready. I'll be in the model."

"Callie's house."

Don's easy remark made the words more real. The model reflected Callie in so many ways. Strong. Beautiful. Attentive to detail.

The idea of selling it made Matt feel guilty, but that was silly. She and Hank had designed the house with no intention of living there. Why should he feel bad?

He climbed into the truck and stared at his phone, knowing Sunday loomed two days away. And Sunday meant church. And Katie, if he went to the White Church at the Bend again.

So he wouldn't. Why would he intentionally encroach on her life? So what that he felt at home the minute he walked in the door. That he eyed the structural problems of the old building, wondering what he could do to help.

He took Route 19 North and hung a right toward Jamison, taking the shortcut back to Cobbled Creek.

As he followed the Park Round curve, Simon Mac-Daniel waved from the driveway of the church.

Matt slowed the truck and rolled down the window. "Hey, Si. What's up?"

Si pulled a worn but thick hoodie closer and grimaced. "I can't believe I'm hoping for snow, but this rain is wreaking havoc with our roof."

Matt thrust his chin toward the church and nodded. "I noticed that. And your interior damage will spread if it doesn't get fixed."

"And money's nonexistent with so many of the congregation heading south this time of year," Si told him. "We've gotten a couple of decent bequests and memoriam donations, but roofing is crazy expensive. We were hoping to hold off until next summer, but I don't think we can."

"I agree. But maybe we can patch the bad spot. Want me to have a look?"

Si stared at him. "You do roofing?"

Matt shrugged. "I own a construction company."

Happiness brightened Si's face. "Providence, right?"

Matt pulled into the drive, climbed out and met the other man's gaze. "You didn't know? Really?"

"Scout's honor," Si promised. "I was just out there, wondering what to do, praying and staring up while realizing I know nothing about constructing buildings…"

"But a fair piece about mending souls," Matt cut in.

"As nice as that sounds," Si replied, "it won't keep us dry when spring blasts us with torrential rains."

"True enough. You got a ladder, Si?"

"Back here."

They set the ladder against the lowest part of the church roof. Matt started up, then paused, looking back. "Thank you for not picking a church with a towering cathedral. Right now small and country seems a whole lot friendlier."

Hinted sadness darkened Si's eyes, passing almost quick enough for Matt to doubt his eyesight. But not quite. "I couldn't agree more." He ascended the ladder behind Matt and hung there while Matt surveyed the roof.

"You're frowning."

"Yup."

"In my experience, frowns equate expensive."

"Yeah. But the good news is, I think I can patch it," Matt told him. "Monday and Tuesday are both supposed to be clear. If I bring a couple of guys by, can we jump up here and get it done for you?"

"I'd be forever in your debt," Si declared.

Matt smiled as he climbed down. "No, you won't, but I wouldn't mind some extra prayers if you've got a mind to. They'd come in handy these next few weeks."

Si clamped a firm hand on his shoulder, his bright blue eyes meeting Matt's. "Consider it done, my friend."

Matt nodded, grateful, then pivoted to climb into the truck, only to stop dead.

Katie approached the two men, and there was no mistaking her look of surprise as she recognized Matt. "Matt, you're back."

He squirmed inside and out. "Katie."

"You're back and you haven't called," she corrected herself, her expression tart.

"I...um..."

"In nearly twenty years," she went on, moving closer, her stride smooth even with the driveway's upgrade. To see her move, he'd never suspect she was handicapped.

"You two know each other." Si offered the interpretation as though heading off trouble, but he needn't have bothered. The look on Katie's face said "storm front coming."

"I thought we did," Katie told Si, her voice signaling otherwise. "But friends don't desert each other when the chips are down. Friends don't abandon one another when things go wrong. Friends—"

"I get it." Matt faced her, feeling unprepared, but wasn't this what he came back for? To have it out with each and every person he'd wronged? Obviously it was Katie's turn.

"So that's it? You stumble across me here, shrug your shoulders and move on?"

He wouldn't do that. Couldn't do that. If God provided this unexpected opportunity, there was obviously a reason. "I have to get back to work right now, but I'd like to talk to you. See you."

Simon shifted beside him, as if wondering about Matt's intent.

"How about tonight?" he continued. "We could meet at that little coffee shop." He jutted his chin toward the café across the green, the artistic sign proclaiming great music, espresso and food beneath a bright yellow flower. "If you're free, that is."

She stared at him with little emotion, but her eyes…

Oh, those eyes said so much. Two decades of anger and disappointment deepened the pale gray to steel. But she nodded and took a broad step away from the truck. "Seven-thirty."

"All right." He turned back toward Simon. "And I'll be sure to come by either Monday or Tuesday with the guys. We'll get that patched up for you."

Simon didn't look quite as happy now, but Matt had enough on his plate. He climbed into the truck, eased it into reverse, and rolled down the driveway, carefully not looking left or right. He didn't need to see Katie's face to read the disappointment there, or Si's to acknowledge the look of question.

He gave up the idea of stopping for coffee, his gut advising him to wait, and headed toward the outskirts of town and Dunnymeade Hill, wondering why he hadn't taken the long way around in the first place.

He knew he had to talk to Katie. Apologize. Set things straight.

But he'd envisioned a more controlled approach. With considerable distance. A phone call, perhaps, or better yet, an email. That's how he'd imagined his first contact with Katie, just enough to give them both time to think. Ponder. Pray.

As he headed into Cobbled Creek, lights in the model told him the Mareks were already at work. The realization calmed him. He'd get through today, then face tonight. Either way, it would be over and done before his head hit a pillow, and he wasn't sure if that was a good thing or bad.

But he'd find out soon enough.

"Morning, boss," Callie called as Matt came through the side entrance of the model. His look appraised the work she'd gotten done. He whistled appreciation, the clean white primer pulling the kitchen's look together.

"You got here early, Cal."

She nodded, concentrating on cutting in along a cabinet's edge. "Couldn't sleep and I wanted this done before the countertop guys come on Monday. Then we can install the sink." She ducked low to do the baseboard, then asked, "What's your time frame on wallboard seaming?"

"Today."

"Want a suggestion?" She looked up at him, unsure of his reaction.

"Maybe."

Callie grinned. "Don's the best seamer around when he's sober and he's been sober for nearly a year."

He stared outside, then sighed. "I've already asked him. He's on his way."

"Really?"

He directed his gaze down to her.

"No argument, no convincing, no appealing to your sensibilities?"

"Yesterday did that."

"Perfect."

"Even when I'm not sure why I should feel guilty about anything concerning Don."

"Wanna talk some more?"

He pulled hardware out of the box and headed toward the living room. "No."

Okay, then.

He popped his head around a few seconds later. "Sorry. Didn't mean to be short with you. None of this is your fault, and—"

"It's okay, Matt. Really."

He looked relieved by her reaction. Sympathy rose from within, a whisper of the little boy lost showing in his eyes.

Gorgeous brown velvet eyes. Deep. Soulful.

"Besides, the walls have ears around here," Matt added.

That was certainly true. "We could grab coffee later," Callie mused.

His look of chagrin said he was busy. Worse, that she'd caught him out. "Another time might be better, huh?" Callie asked, her mind going back to the message from Reenie.

Her voice must have said more than her words because Matt poked his head around the corner again. "I'm not dating anyone, Cal. And if you've got something to ask, darlin', just spit it out." He flashed that smile again, the one that said he'd read her hesitation and countered it. "And just to straighten things out, Reenie is the gal who does doll-up for me. She sweeps, mops, wipes things down, makes sure everything's pristine before buyers walk in the front door.

She's in her fifties, married and has four grandchildren. Although her macadamia brownies *are* a temptation."

Callie sent him a scathing look, but he'd already ducked back to his side of the half wall. Just as well. She had work to do and conversation might pull her off-task.

"But I'd like to grab coffee with you," he called back, sounding more serious this time, "Talk about things. But not tonight. I, um…"

"Have plans." Callie filled in the blank without looking up.

"Yes."

The guy was entitled to a life, right? And what business was it of hers what he did on a cold, wet Friday night? "Let me know when. As long as Jake's taken care of, we're good."

"Thanks, Cal." Relief colored his tone which meant he didn't realize she was quietly stewing on the other side of the wall, a ridiculous fact because they both understood the boundaries they'd established.

Maybe she'd be better off returning to the diner. Working for Matt paid better, but dealing with these rising emotions put her at risk.

Why? Her conscience prodded. *You're here to do a job. You need money. And Matt's okay with the parameters, except when he's kissing you.*

That kiss. That one sweet, gentle kiss, a glimpse of what could be.

"Mom! I'm here!"

Reality pushed her wandering thoughts aside. Jake was her certainty. Matt understood and respected that. He'd said so. And God had blessed her in so many ways already. Even now, with losing the subdivision, they'd gained a friend and good employer in Matt Cavanaugh. Bad had turned into good. Callie was smart enough to recognize that.

"Hey, bud, can you keep going on those cabinet doors for me?" Matt called.

"Sure, Matt! Is it okay if The General comes in?"

"Jake. Wet dog." Callie scooted back and frowned. "Really?"

Matt's cell phone rang, a straightforward sound, no fancy ring tones or songs. Callie liked that. He scanned the phone, frowned and headed to the garage, his look saying he wasn't getting a signal in the house, and the garage was a quieter choice as Hank and Jim's arrival added to the noise of doggie feet and Jake's excitement.

Besides, a guy was entitled to a little privacy. Callie refocused her attention on the walls, ignoring pinpricks of jealousy. She had a life. So did he. End of story.

Matt picked up the call in the garage and sighed relief when Mary Kay Hammond's voice came through loud and clear. "Mary Kay, good morning. You're working today?"

The Realtor laughed. "Make money when you can, I say. And while this never happens on a major holiday weekend, I got a call this morning from someone interested in Cobbled Creek. They're in town for the weekend, and they're coming by my office later to look at plans. They'd like to stop by tomorrow and see the model."

"They know it's not done, right?"

"They don't care. They're moving here from downstate and Cobbled Creek reminded them of the Catskills. They're enamored."

Matt laughed. "Enamored is good. What time tomorrow?"

"Ten-thirty. We're looking at a couple of existing homes as well, but these folks seem to prefer a new build."

Matt understood the difference. Some people cherished the feel of old wood, past times. Others? Nothing but new would do. And those were the ones he hoped to court with Cobbled Creek. "See you then. And they know we can upgrade any way they want, right?"

Mary Kay laughed. "I've got it covered, Matt. You build. I'll sell. And I won't promise them anything you can't deliver, okay? And we'll adjust the pricing accordingly."

"Excellent." Mary Kay's promise sounded light, but Matt had worked with salespeople who didn't have a clue what upgrades meant to the contractor's bottom line. Mary Kay? She got it, which is why she still had a business when others bellied-up with the housing downfall.

"I'll see you tomorrow, then."

"We'll be there."

Matt headed back inside, whistling softly. Callie looked up at him and smiled. "You look happier."

He shrugged, sheepish. "A prospective buyer coming tomorrow."

"Really?" Callie grinned, no hint of envy or remorse shading her features. "Matt, that's wonderful."

"It sure is," cut in Hank as he rounded the corner from the family room. "On a holiday weekend. And this time of year. I figured we wouldn't see anybody until February."

Matt had thought the same thing. He'd hoped for earlier, but knew it was unlikely.

"They interested in the model?" Hank asked.

Matt shook his head. "I don't know." He wanted to sneak a peek at Callie to see if that bothered her, but he'd already figured out that Callie was adept at painting on a game face as needed. "They're exploring their options."

"It would be wonderful to lock in a contract," Callie said from the floor. She stretched to finish the last corner, and Matt thought how nice it was to have her there, keeping the bottom line in sight. Callie's pragmatism about getting a job done kept things focused. Balanced.

"I'll do a really good job on the doors," Jake promised.

Matt rubbed Jake's head as he went by. "Thanks, bud. Oh, and here's Don," he added as the aging car pulled into the drive. "He's going to start seaming today."

Hank slowed Matt's progress with a hand to his

arm. The older man didn't say a word, but the approval in his eyes told Matt he'd done well.

But because flashes of the unresolved scene with Katie were fresh in his mind, Matt could only hope Hank was right.

Hank tipped his head toward the driveway. "This will be good for him. He's having a rough go right now."

"Due to?" Matt scrutinized Hank's calm look, then thought back. Don's pallor. His words. "He's sick?"

"I can't say more, but it's treatable. Still, a hard road when you're alone."

"Cancer."

Hank confirmed nothing, but Matt read his face. "Is he healthy enough to do this?"

"Best thing in the world for him. Purpose. Focus. He's never been much of one for leaning on God no matter how much I yammer at him."

Matt had no trouble envisioning that. "Thanks, Hank."

Hank sent him a cautionary look as he moved toward the stairs. "Between us, okay?"

"I hear ya."

Don pushed through the side entry and paused, inspecting what they'd done. "Nice." He turned and saw Matt there, and the tentative smile punched another little hole into the hard core of Matt's heart. "This is beautiful, Matt."

"Thanks. Hank's upstairs." He jerked a thumb toward the stairway. "He can get you started."

Don headed up, looking more confident with a box of tools in his hand. What had Hank said? Purpose. Focus.

Matt hadn't realized what wonderful gifts they were, but seeing the quick difference in Don's gait? His expression?

That combination made Matt glad he'd manned up and stopped by Don's place. Now if only things went well with Katie.

But recalling the look on her face that morning, that didn't fall into the realm of likely.

Chapter Eleven

"You goin' out, Matt?" Jake asked as Matt descended the stairs that evening.

Matt shrugged into his jacket and nodded. "For a little while."

"Oh." The boy's chin dropped.

"What's up, bud?"

"Nothing." Jake shook his head and Callie wasn't sure whether to chastise him or kiss him for making Matt feel guilty. She'd decide that later. For right now she folded laundry while the dishwasher hummed and Jake gazed up at Matt with hero-worship eyes and a quivering jaw. "See ya."

Matt hesitated, torn.

Callie caved. "Jake, Matt spends lots of time with you. It's not nice to make him feel guilty for going out."

"Sorry, Matt."

Matt stooped low. "I'll be here tomorrow, bud. And we can wage war along the Pacific Rim if you want."

"I have to go to a birthday party tomorrow." Jake

droned the words as if attendance was a fate worse than death.

Matt moved back, surprised. "Birthday parties rock. Ice cream. Cake. Games."

"For a girl."

"Oh."

"Yeah." Jake looked up, woebegone. "Mom said I have to go."

"Well…" Matt wavered, then nodded. "We've got to be polite."

"To girls?"

"Especially to girls."

"Jake, we've had this discussion," Callie cut in. "You're going, you will be polite, and Matt's going to be late for whatever it is he's doing tonight." And looking wonderful, Callie added silently, but then, this was Matt. He looked great no matter what, but tonight he was freshly shaved and had on a classy black leather bomber jacket.

Gorgeous.

"Be good tonight, okay?" Matt ruffled Jake's hair as he stood.

"I will."

"Good." He shifted his attention to Callie. "I don't know how long I'll be…"

"Grown-ups don't have curfews," Callie assured him, hoping her smile wasn't stretched too tight. "You have a life, Matt. It's okay to lead it."

He faced her across the table, his hands fisted.

She couldn't decipher the tense look in his eyes, or read the clench of his jaw, but instinct told her he might need help. She moved around the table slowly, holding his gaze, needing to reassure him. She stopped just short of him and reached up a hand to cup his cheek, his jaw. "If God is with us, who can be against us?"

His eyes softened. He leaned his cheek into her hand, just enough to send a message of gratitude, the feel of his skin warm beneath her palm. He smelled of pricey aftershave and clean leather, and when he smiled at her it was all she could do not to melt.

"Thanks, Cal."

"See ya."

He nodded, sent her mouth a look that said he wished they were alone, then moved toward the door.

He wasn't whistling. And she recognized the haunted look in his eyes, the stolid set of his face. She went to the door and gazed out, Matt's taillights growing smaller as he headed toward town. "God, bless him. Whatever this is, keep him safe. Sound. Peaceful. Help him bridge this gap, dear Lord. He's such a good, gentle man."

"Mom, can we start decorating inside tonight?"

Callie sighed and shook her head. "No, kid. I'm beat. But tomorrow, yes. However," she added, seeing his look of disappointment, "we can get the stuff out tonight and then we're ready for tomorrow. We can probably get a bunch of things done before the birthday party."

His smile uplifted her. Such a little thing to decorate for the holidays. And Jake's smile?

Totally a gift from God.

* * *

Matt paced the sidewalk in front of the café, half wishing Katie would stand him up.

She didn't. She headed his way from across the street, the village quiet, even on Black Friday. He stepped forward, not sure where to begin. Hello seemed appropriate. "Hey. Thanks for coming."

She studied his face as if looking for something, then shrugged. "I didn't want to."

"I know."

"But I had to," she went on as though he hadn't spoken. "Because *I* don't want to be the person who walks away and never looks back."

Matt felt the direct shot. He jerked his head toward the door. "Let's go in. If we're at a back table, we won't get overheard by too many."

A tiny smile flashed momentarily. "This is Jamison. All it takes is one."

True, but Matt wondered if that was such a bad thing. If a person chose honor and goodness, would they care what was said about them? Of course not.

Which meant small towns were fine as long as you behaved yourself. He glanced around once they were seated in the Green Room, surprised by the flurry of customers. "I thought it would be quiet."

"Not on weekend nights. People come in for the music," she trailed a look to a pair of guitar players settling in near the fireplace, "and the food. And the coffee is marvelous."

"Katie, hey." The taller guitarist moved their way,

comfortable in the close-knit setting. "Did you bring your fiddle?"

She laughed. "It's at home, Cedric. It's not my night to play."

"Impromptu becomes you, Katie girl."

Katie leaned forward and gestured toward Matt. "Cedric MacDaniel, this is Matt Cavanaugh."

The man turned his way and extended his hand. "The builder."

"Yes."

"I'm Simon's brother. He told me you were coming by to patch his roof."

Matt nodded. "Hopefully we can get it taken care of this week."

"I roofed my way through college," Cedric told him. "If you need help, I'm available on weekends."

"Thanks."

Katie turned as Cedric headed back across the room. "He and Simon are fraternal twins."

"They're not from here."

"No." Katie shook her head, gave the waiter her order, paused while Matt did the same, then continued, "Simon took over the White Church ministry, then Cedric followed. Their parents were killed in the attack on the World Trade Center."

"Seriously?"

"Yeah." Katie nodded, rimmed her water glass with one finger, then sighed. "Simon was an associate pastor in Connecticut. Cedric was working in the financial district, but several blocks up."

"So he was right there." Matt couldn't fathom it,

to be on hand and know your parents worked in the towers that came crashing down. "That's rough."

Katie turned her attention full back to him. "Rough stuff happens, Matt. To most of us. Then we pick up the pieces and move on, which you've obviously done."

Her tone didn't make it sound like a compliment. "I hope so." He paused, drew a breath and waded in. "I came back to apologize, Katie."

"And build houses."

Her cryptic tone said she wasn't buying his apology theory.

"That, too, but the reason I bought Cobbled Creek was to help make amends. To make something pretty out of threatened property."

"And make money."

"Let's hope." He met her gaze. "You don't stay in business if you don't make money."

"Or maybe," she said, leaning forward, her eyes locked on his, "You came back to show everyone how successful you are. How industrious. The bad boy returns and waves his success in the face of the people who wronged him."

"No one wronged me," he corrected her. "I was the one who messed up. I ruined a lot of things in my day, but the worst…" He shifted his attention away, then brought it back, reluctant. "The worst was what I did to you."

"Not calling me? Not coming to see me? Not writing?" She sat back, letting one rhythmic finger tap against the table top.

"Hurting you." He waved toward her leg. "Causing your injuries. Driving drunk and stupid."

"So seeing me is your reparation?"

Matt frowned. "Katie, it's..."

"Because, for your information, Matt Cavanaugh, totally ignoring me after the accident was way more painful than losing a limb ever thought of being."

"Katie—"

"Do you know how long I was in that hospital? In rehab? How I longed for a friendly face?"

"Your father wouldn't let anyone near you, Katie. You know that."

"Then you should have tried harder, Matt."

He scowled, wishing she was wrong.

"You let shame and guilt rule you. And you didn't even help the public defender when your court case came up. You could have pleaded down, you could have told the judge about your life, you could have helped yourself and maybe lessened your sentence..."

"I didn't deserve a lesser sentence. If anything, I should have served longer."

"Shut up."

He sat back, amazed.

"You." She half stood and shook a finger at him, her expression tough and tart. "You acted like a sacrificial lamb, like the whole thing was your fault, like Pete, Joe and I didn't have options. We had choices, Matt. We were stupid drunk just like you, and it was only by chance you were driving. The accident happened because four of us were stupid. Not one. And it was more hurtful to lose your friendship than to lose my leg, and if you think I'm not one-hundred-percent serious about that, then you don't know me."

Her words hit home, but was she right or sugar-coating a horrible circumstance? "I was driving."

"Only because Joe got sick," she reminded him. "Matt, listen." She edged forward again.

Matt leaned back. "Are you going to hit me?"

The tiny smile he glimpsed outside returned. "I'm tempted, but no. We were young. Stupid. We stole that car and went drinking and driving late at night, but each of us made a conscious choice to be there. We were just as wrong as you. But you…" she reached out and smoothed a hand to his face. "You took it on the chin for us."

"Katie, you lost your leg," he reminded her, hating that she felt sorry for him when he'd cost her so much. "I maimed you because I was reckless. I can't forgive myself for that."

"Well, then you're still stupid," she told him, but her voice was softer. Gentler. "Because I forgave you a long time ago. And I forgave my father for being so tough and critical," she added, wrinkling her nose, an expression he remembered as though it was yesterday. "Although I try to avoid him as much as possible, and that's tough in a small town, but Matt," she bent farther forward, her tone strong but sincere, "our families were a piece of work for different reasons. God doesn't hold that against us. He knows kids make mistakes and need forgiveness. It's what we do as adults that counts. And did you ever stop to think the accident happened for a reason? That it might have been the wake-up call we needed?" She accepted her latte from the waiter and paused as Matt took his coffee.

"We were on the road to early graves," she continued. "That accident put the brakes on. Made us grow up. Now we've all got successful careers. Pete's got two beautiful kids and is a grocery manager at Tops. Joe's a mechanic at a big car dealership in Olean, and loves it."

"He always loved tinkering under a hood," Matt mused.

"And you've done well, Matt," she reminded him. "You've served your country, you've built a business, you're honest and upright."

"How do you know all this?"

She scoffed a laugh. "The web. I've watched you along the way, just checking to see if you were okay."

"I am." Saying the words out loud, Matt almost believed them. "I was nervous about meeting you."

"Me, too. But mostly mad," Katie added, grinning.

"I saw that, which might have been the source of my fear," Matt admitted. "You look wonderful."

"You, too. And I love that you've taken over Cobbled Creek," she added. "Not because I didn't want the Mareks successful," she hastened to add. "But just because they looked so sad that the whole thing fell apart. Callie is about one of the toughest, strongest gals I know..."

"She's incredible. I don't know what I'd do without her," Matt agreed. Something in his tone deepened Katie's smile.

"She is. And she works so hard at everything she does, and her little boy?" Katie lifted her shoulders. "He's wonderful even though his father walked out on him when he was a baby."

"A feeling I can relate to," Matt noted. "But Jake seems fine."

"He does," Katie agreed, "but it's got to bother him. Look back at you and me when we were young. There was a lot we didn't let show."

She was right. They'd hidden their emotional wounds, but things surfaced when they acted out as young teens. "I can't believe the dumb things we did."

"Me neither. And if I'm ever a mom," Katie continued, "I want to be a great one. With a wonderful husband who's committed to God and his family. And a good dog."

"You always loved dogs."

"Still do." Wistfulness softened her expression. "But I can't have one in my apartment in Wellsville and I'm never there anyway. I work as a nurse at Jones Memorial, play violin for the church and teach skiing on winter weekends."

Skiing? Matt didn't shield the surprise on his face quick enough and her finger waved again. "Don't make assumptions about what my life is like, Matt. You see me as broken, but I prefer to think of it as just another challenge. An extra mogul in the down-hill slopes of life."

"You're incredible."

"Well." She patted her leg as the waiter brought a

serving of spinach and artichoke dip with a side of pita chips. "Computerized prosthetics are a wonder these days. And they're using me to test new apparatus that responds to the brain."

"Your brain tells the leg what to do?"

"And the leg does it." She grinned and grabbed a chip. "Not quite as perfect as the real deal, but amazing, nonetheless. So yeah, I ski, I bike, I run, I play, I work." She reached out and held his hand, her fingers soft and warm. "I decided that I needed to work harder, better and longer to conquer those early demons. So I did. Same as you."

He gripped her hand, grateful for her forgiveness. Her friendship. "I'm proud of you, Katie."

"You, too." She lifted her chin and smiled as the first notes of Cedric's guitar sounded. "And being here with you on a Thanksgiving weekend? Laying all the old drama to rest?" She leaned forward and kissed his cheek. "Thank you, Matt. God bless you."

God had blessed him, Matt realized. In so many ways. He smiled and raised her fingers for a kiss. "You, too, Katie."

Jill Calhoun's Facebook pic shouldn't have hurt so much, but it did, and that only meant Callie'd been careless.

But the picture, sent from Jill's cell phone, showing Katie Bascomb kissing Matt, looking sweet, blonde and beautiful made Callie recognize her vulnerability. Obviously she'd misinterpreted Matt's looks, his words, that soul-searching kiss, but was that his fault or hers?

His, she decided. Men shouldn't toy with a woman's affections, and a single mom to boot? Shameful.

Her phone rang a short while later, Jill's number in the display. When she didn't pick up, a text appeared. "Is this the hunk working with you? No wonder you gave up your shifts at the diner! When opportunity knocks…" Jill had inserted a smiley face. "A smart girl's gotta be around to open the door."

Not so smart when the guy's off kissing someone else, Callie mused. She headed to bed, not wanting to be awake when Matt came home.

This isn't his home, her conscience stabbed. *It's a convenient place to stay. And that's it.*

The internal warning was just what Callie needed, a reminder to step back. Maintain distance. Being independent worked for her. She'd be foolish to forget that. Relationships meant risk, and her responsibility to Jake curtailed those opportunities. And because Matt was also her boss, and Dad's boss, well…

Time to revert back to what she'd known all along: Don't date the boss. Or flirt with him. Or daydream about forever afters in sweet stone-faced Capes with twinkle lights welcoming you home at Christmas.

She fell asleep with a headache. One that was her fault for letting herself get silly. She knew better, and she'd apply the brakes now. That was best all around.

Knowing that didn't help the headache, though.

Chapter Twelve

The smell of fresh coffee roused her early the next morning. She yawned, stretched, then remembered.

Katie and Matt. Kissing.

The headache re-erupted, full-blown.

Ibuprofen for breakfast in that case. She got dressed and headed downstairs, quiet.

"Hey." Matt's quick smile and pleased salute strengthened the headache's hold. Why had she let herself be so stupid?

"Morning." She crossed the room, poured coffee and fixed it in the kitchen, looking anywhere but at Matt.

"You okay, Cal?" His evident concern only strengthened the steel rod along her backbone.

"A little headache. Nothing major."

"Are you getting sick?" He stood and came her way, his closeness offsetting her planned evasive maneuvers.

A plan she was losing because he smelled marvelous. She took a broad step back. "I'm fine. Probably just slept funny."

"Do you want me to rub your shoulders? Your neck? Is your pillow too soft?"

Like she was about to discuss her pillow with Matt Cavanaugh. She shrugged him off, grabbed her lined flannel and headed for the door. "It'll work itself out. And I want to get the model cleared up before those buyers arrive. I'll see you over there."

His gaze followed her out the door, a marine's battlefield assessment. By the time he joined her in the model, she'd applied a finishing coat to the kitchen walls and was ready to hang kitchen lighting fixtures.

"Looks good."

Two words. That's all he said as he walked through, heading into the family room to apply trim. And his tone said they were words he'd have said to any worker, anytime, a casual compliment with nothing else implied, which was exactly what she wanted. So why did it feel so bad?

"Nice kitchen." Don came through the side door next. He examined the kitchen's layout and faced Callie. He smiled his appreciation. "You did a great job with this, Callie."

"Thanks, Don. Most of it was already in the plans."

He harrumphed. "I saw the original layout, remember? And the way you added the plate rack above, the spindles along the far edge, the double pantry…?" He took a contemplative sip of coffee. "Your mother would have loved this."

His words smoothed her prickled feelings, like extrafine sandpaper on wild-grained oak. "You think?"

"Oh, yeah. All this cupboard space, so neat and pretty? She'd have had a ball in a kitchen like this."

"Good." Callie finished the last strip along the upper edge and turned to step back onto the ladder. Her toe caught the lip of the cupboard fascia. She held a wet paintbrush in one hand and a can of paint in the other. No way was she about to spill paint on these new cupboards with people coming in two hours.

She tipped, knowing the fall was inevitable, wishing she'd stayed focused.

"I've got you."

Matt's strong arms braced her, holding her steady, his welcome words emotionally painful. He held on while she unhooked her foot, then asked, "Don, can you take the paint?"

"Sure."

Callie set the can in Don's hand, then the brush. She stepped back onto the ladder, feeling Matt's hand at her waist, wondering if he'd been this nice to Katie last night, wishing Jill never sent the photo.

But a part of her thanked God for the wake-up call. She'd promised herself no more missteps with men and romance. Falling for Matt?

Big mistake?

"Are you okay?"

Strong, rugged hands gripped her shoulders. And she thought she heard a slight tremor in his voice. *Don't look up.*

Too late. He released one shoulder and tipped

her chin, scrutinizing her. "Did you pull anything? Sprain anything?"

"Besides my pride? No."

A soft smile brightened his worried features. "Pride goeth before the fall," he quipped.

She tried to ease back.

He didn't let go. And Don had disappeared upstairs, leaving them alone. "You scared me."

Yeah, well... "Glad you happened by, marine."

He studied her like he had before she left the house, then shrugged. "I'm confused. You're mad at me and I don't know why. We haven't seen each other since last night and you were fine when I left to meet Katie."

She flinched. An "aha" moment widened his eyes. "You're mad because I met Katie for coffee?"

She pulled back, harder this time. "Matt, it's like I told Jake last night. You have a life. You need to lead it. Living with us is a convenience, I get that, and we don't want to make you uncomfortable. Do what you've got to do and it will all work out."

She might have pulled back firmly, but her strength didn't come close to matching his, which made her gesture futile. "You're jealous."

"No."

He had the audacity to smile and that nearly got him taken out at the knees. "Yes, but I don't get why," he mused, not letting her go, almost enjoying this. One quick look at his face said there was no "almost" about it. "First Reenie. Now Katie. You got trust issues going on, Cal?"

She did, thanks to a cheating husband and a lousy self-image, but that was none of his concern. "I trust you for a paycheck, Matt. Nothing more. Got it?"

"Got it." He released her then, but the twinkle in his eye said more. Way more. "And I forgot how quickly information travels around here, so the next time I meet an old friend, I'll employ full disclosure up front, okay?"

"No need." She slapped the top on the paint can with more vigor than needed, droplets of paint spattering the subfloor. She growled, chagrined.

He leaned down, close. Very close. "You're awful cute when you're mad. You know that?"

Hank and Jake's arrival warded off her reply, and she spent the next two hours wiping, polishing, vacuuming and sweeping. When Mary Kay pulled in with the prospective buyers, the crew slipped out the back door. They aimed for the Marek house to give the Realtor time to show the people around. Matt hung back to meet the buyers, but he managed to catch Callie's arm as she left. She bit her lower lip, determined to say nothing. Silence seemed best at the moment.

Matt gestured to the cleaned-up model, his gaze teasing. He leaned in, dropped her a wink and drawled, "Reenie couldn't have done it better, Cal. Thank you."

"You're not funny."

"Oh, I am." He softened his grip on her arm and sent her mouth a wistful look. "But I'm sorry you misunderstood about Katie. I'll explain it soon, okay?" He glanced around the work space and shrugged. "I keep meaning to but we've been busy." He shifted his attention to the guys heading toward the Marek house. "And we're never alone."

That was certainly true.

"Soon. Promise." He smiled at her, his eyes sending a message her heart longed to hear, but was it the longing or the message that ruled the moment? Callie couldn't be sure, and until she was, she was safer maintaining distance.

The chatter of voices redirected her attention. "I'll head home. Make fresh coffee. Go schmooze these people with your charm and expertise."

"Expertise will get me further," Matt replied.

Not necessarily. He might be a first-class builder. She'd witnessed that. But his charm?

Off the charts. And that's what worried her most.

She gave the house one last look as the voices grew louder, hoping they'd love it, praying they'd see merit in her changes and upgrades, while a part of her hated to see it go. "Good luck."

"Thanks." Matt squeezed her arm and straightened his shoulders, heading back in. "I'll be over shortly."

"Or call if this takes longer than you expected. I'll fix you a cup and bring it over."

"Thanks, Callie."

She told herself she was just being nice, that she'd hope for anyone's success the same way, but the Marek–Cavanaugh building connection had her personally invested. Good or bad, they'd put heart and soul into this venture, and today's viewing could signal success or failure. She sent him a confident nod and turned toward home, wondering what they'd gotten themselves into. "Anytime, boss."

She doesn't want to sell the model.

The realization struck him as he closed the family room door.

Callie's personal investment in this house showed throughout, even though it wasn't quite done, and her quick look of longing?

That gripped his heart, but they'd built the model to sell, right? So why was this so hard?

"Matt, you're here." Mary Kay's warm greeting inspired his smile as she came through the garage entrance followed by a thirty-something couple. They looked nice. Normal. And as they stepped in, the woman grabbed her husband's arm, delighted. "Look at these maple cabinets, Ben. Aren't they gorgeous?"

"Very nice." He stuck out a hand to Matt. "Ben Wiseman. And this is my wife, Chloe, the woman who ignored my instructions about not showing how much you like the house because it drives the price up."

Matt laughed, shook his hand, and then Chloe's. "I've wired the walls to record conversation, actually. That way I can access every exclamation and adjust the price upward accordingly."

"Clever technology."

Matt grinned. "We do what we can."

Mary Kay linked her arm through his. "Matt is a marine. He did multiple tours overseas and when he got home he worked night and day to build this business. And by buying Cobbled Creek from the Marek family…"

The couple nodded, obviously up-to-date on the subdivision's history.

"Matt's been working *with* the Mareks to stay true to the original design and specifications."

"Isn't that tough?" Ben asked Matt. "Working with the family that lost this?"

Matt shook his head. "I'd have thought so, too, but no. It's been wonderful. And they live across the road, so they'll be your neighbors if you decide to live here. And you couldn't ask for better ones anywhere."

"Kids?" Chloe asked.

"A boy. Eight years old. His name's Jake."

"The same age as our Jordan." Chloe surveyed the kitchen. "And I love the ratio of cupboard and pantry space to work space in this kitchen."

"That's Callie Marek's doing," Matt told them. "She's got a great eye."

"We loved the layout of the neighborhood," Ben confessed. "And I probably shouldn't tell you that, but the minute we saw it, it reminded us of the vacation spot Chloe's parents had in the Catskills."

"The way you've nestled the homes into the hillside drew us," added Chloe.

Matt would have to thank Hank and Callie for their hard work. Sure, he'd come in at the last moment to pull things together, but money and timing couldn't fix poor initial planning, and the welcoming look of Cobbled Creek attested to that.

But now it was time to let Mary Kay do her job. Matt shook hands again and headed for the door, cell phone in hand. "If you need me, call, but I want to get out of your way so you feel free to examine things fully."

"Thanks, Matt." Mary Kay's nod said his timing was perfect, making him wish he could do that in all facets of his life.

Hah.

He headed toward the Marek house, his gaze drawn to the plywood Holy Family staked in the lawn. Simple. Austere. Poignant.

Callie and Hank didn't have much, but faith and love shined in everything they did. They took care of each other, the way a family should. Callie'd grown up with one parent. Jake was doing the same. Matt had been left virtually parentless at a young age, and for just a moment he wondered if the American dream of Mom, Dad and kids living together was an illusion. A shadow of reality, an old truth.

It doesn't have to be, son.

Grandpa's sage words washed over him.

It's all about choices. Good and bad. Every step of the way.

Grandpa was right. Eyeing the Marek house, Matt recognized the growing feeling inside himself. The way his heart had stopped beating when Callie nearly fell. The way it ramped up pace when she smiled at him. How she managed to capture his heart by cupping his cheek.

He wanted to be her helper, her protector. Her knight in shining armor.

But that meant he had to set the record straight, and people would talk after seeing him with Katie last night. They'd reminisce and wonder out loud. Which meant he had to tell Callie first.

"Did they like the house, Matt?" Jake spouted the question the moment Matt stepped through the door.

Matt picked him up, tossed him into a fireman's hold and noogied the boy's head while Jake laughed in glee. "They seemed to, bud. But I had to get out of there and let Mary Kay do her job."

"What's that mean?"

"Schmooze 'em," explained Hank.

Jake frowned, confused.

"Mary Kay's job is to point out the good things about a house so people want to buy it."

"Although nothing about Cobbled Creek needs glossing over," declared Don.

"Absolutely not," exclaimed Buck, who must have joined the group after they'd walked to the Mareks'.

"It's beautiful just the way it is," threw in Jim roundly, adding his support.

"You sound like a bunch of pom-pom wavin' cheerleaders," Hank grumped, but his grin of appreciation showed his true feelings. "Matt, Buck brought bagels." He waved a hand toward the counter.

"Sounds good. Thanks, Buck." He turned toward Callie. "Weren't you and Jake going to start decorating?"

She nodded. "I figured now is the perfect time so those people can wander at will with Mary Kay, then I can work on the model this afternoon while Jake's at the birthday party."

"Good. I'll grab a couple of these," he took two bagels from the counter and wrapped them in a double paper towel, "and we can head back. Get some stuff done on number twenty-three."

Did he just glance wistfully at the stack of boxes? Like a little boy lost, gazing in a Christmas window?

No.

He headed toward the door, bagels in hand, almost hurrying, as if he couldn't wait to leave. *Or because he badly longed to stay.*

"Matt, can you help us?" Callie's voice stretched high, nerves showing.

"Really?" He turned, caught off guard, as if making sure he heard correctly.

"Sure, Matt!"

"I mean, if you're too busy…" Callie went on, offering him a way out. If he wanted one, that is.

"He's not, are you, Matt?" Jake implored. "Because you can work this afternoon when I'm at the party, right?"

"I can," Matt told him, his voice deep and easy. "Happy to do that, bud."

"Matt loved helping with Christmas when he was little," Don added.

A shot of pain darkened Matt's gaze, but Callie drew him forward, ready to fix old wrongs. Now was a time for hope. Happiness. Health. "Good, then you're experienced." She grinned at him and directed him to a spot on the couch. "You sit here and open these." She slid a pile of boxes to his left as the guys grabbed hats and gloves.

"The guys and I will start getting those plumbing lines laid in number twenty-three, Matt," Hank said smoothly, "because we can't finish those last two roofs until the weather clears. And then Don can head back to seaming the model once it's clear of people."

"I love plumbing," Buck announced. He headed for the door. "You sure it won't bother the folks looking around?"

Matt shook his head. "They know we have to work. And they've had more than a half hour already."

"And time's money," added Hank, but he winked Matt's way, "although we wouldn't mind nailing down that first contract."

"That would be wonderful," Matt agreed.

Chapter Thirteen

As the aging but earnest military crew trooped out, Matt turned, catching Callie's look. "A little obvious?"

Callie smiled. "Blatantly, but sweet."

Matt snorted as Jake dragged a box closer. "What soldier wants to be called sweet?" he asked, making a face.

Too late he realized his mistake as he caught Callie's look. "Present company excluded, of course."

"Uh-huh."

"So what's first?" He surveyed the boxes and let Callie take the lead.

"The manger scene goes on the painted chest alongside the fireplace."

"This box." Jake pulled a smaller one front and center. "And this one," he added, shifting another one forward.

"Great. Let me just grab a—"

"Gotcha covered, marine." Callie slipped alongside Matt and handed off a cup of coffee, fragrant and steaming hot, her thoughtfulness curling around his heart, the scent of coffee, Callie and a hint of wood smoke feeling like he'd come home to a greeting card Christmas. He leaned forward and bumped foreheads with her, ever so gently. "Thank you."

Her smile said so much. Too much? He hoped not. Prayed not. "You're welcome."

"So." He sat on the floor, balanced his coffee on a side table and opened the first box. "I'll unpack while you guys direct. Is that okay?"

"It's great, Matt!" Jake grinned in wide enthusiasm, his bright blue eyes different from his mother's jade green, but his gentle joy at grasping life? That was Callie all the way.

Matt reached into the first box and withdrew a rugged barnlike structure. "The stable."

"Which might have been a cave," Jake explained solemnly. "People aren't really sure, but we know they kept animals there."

"History lesson noted." Matt smiled up at him and handed him an unwrapped camel.

"These guys go over here," Jake continued, intent on detail. He moved the camel off to the side. "The wise men didn't get to see Jesus for a while, but we like to remember their visit at Christmas so we include them."

Matt angled a glance up to Callie. "Does he get his love of history from you?"

She sent him a dubious look. "Dad's been teaching him history since birth. And Jake eats it up. I'm lucky I remember breakfast."

"I get it." He unwrapped more figures and smiled

as Jake set them carefully around the rough, wooden stable, frequently stepping back to see if they were placed just right. "The fussiness he gets from you," Matt observed, grinning, a few minutes later.

"I prefer to call it attention to detail," Callie shot back as she attempted to unravel a tangled set of twinkle lights. "Which is why that model kitchen might just sell a house for you."

"For us," Matt corrected.

She looked embarrassed but pleased to be included.

"I mean it, Cal. I couldn't have gotten this done without a great crew and having your family on hand. And the guys." Matt winked at Jake as he handed off a statue of Joseph. "Made all the difference in the world."

"We could just all work together forever," Jake announced, serious and cute. "That way we can build houses and everyone has a job."

"Jake."

"Great idea." Matt handed Jake a slightly chipped gray donkey and sent a lazy smile Callie's way. "We'll have to see how things go, okay?"

"Okay!" He grinned as Matt continued helping, the easy act of unwrapping history binding in its simplicity.

Callie finished unraveling the lights, plugged them in, then groaned.

Matt hid a chuckle behind a cough. "Might want to test 'em first the next time."

When she turned to scowl at him he tugged her

down beside him, pointing to the second box. "Let's do these together. Then the lights. Is there garland for the mantel?"

"Yes."

"Lovely."

"And Mom always puts Christmas cards up there, and candles," Jake explained. "It's real pretty."

"Like your mom."

Jake turned, suspicious. "Are you guys getting mushy?"

"No," Callie said.

"Well…" Matt grinned at her, tweaked her nose, then handed Jake the next figure. She blushed, and in that heightened color Matt read the possibility of a future he'd denied himself, the thought of working with the Mareks, coming home to this family, a gift like no other. He watched Callie hand up a lamb to Jake, then asked, "How about if you and I do some shopping tonight?"

"Can I come?" Jake asked instantly.

"May I," Callie corrected. She shook her head, chin down, and continued to unwrap figures. "We probably shouldn't."

"Sure we should." Matt stretched across her and tugged the box of lights closer. "Jake can stay with Hank and you and I can get our Christmas shopping done."

"I'll be good," Jake wheedled.

"You'll be in bed," Matt corrected him mildly. He gave a lock of Callie's hair a tug. "What do you think? Good idea?"

*　*　*

Instinct had told her to say no after seeing Matt and Katie canoodling at a cozy table in the acoustic café. Shopping with Matt might possibly be the *worst* idea she'd ever heard, so why did she say yes?

Because you're a sucker for the little boy you see behind the rugged marine.

Either way, here they were at the mall later that night, the sweet glow of Christmas lights framing windows and doors, their bright presence climbing columns and archways. "This must look like fairyland to a kid like Jake," Matt mused as they walked through the food court surrounded by mouth-watering smells. Soft notes of Christmas music floated from a keyboard player centered amid the tables.

"You never came to the mall at Christmas when you were a kid?" Callie asked. One look at his face answered that. "Then I'm glad to be with you this time," she told him and hugged his arm.

"You think Jake's mad at us because we wouldn't let him come?"

Honesty was the best policy. *Most times.* "I think Jake has a wicked case of hero worship and thinks you're the best thing since sliced bread."

"No argument there." Matt grinned at her. "The boy's smart. So what are we shopping for?"

"Not much." She paused and faced him, determined to be up front, although admitting her limits made them seem more constraining. "My budget is small. Think miniscule. So is Dad's. Jake needs a new bike, so that's it. And some new socks and art supplies for school. Crayons, markers, cool pencils, tablets, et cetera."

Matt accepted what she said easily. "So if I got him some miniature cars and trucks, would that be okay?"

"He'd love that."

"And maybe his first power drill?"

"Matt—"

"And I could build him a workbench."

"Stop!" She put two fingers against his mouth to shush him, and tried unsuccessfully to ignore the feel of his face, his mouth against her skin. Right then she wished she had soft, feminine fingers, uncalloused, unworn, the silky-soft skin she saw advertised everywhere. And despite her attempts to heal the roughened skin with creams, her fingers showed the effects of working in cold, dry conditions on a steady basis.

Matt caught her hand, kissed it, smiled and said, "Okay, I'm a little excited. I've never shopped for a kid before. Maybe I should do the tool thing for him instead of cars."

"He does have some cars already," Callie agreed, trying to ignore the feel of her hand clasped in his and failing. "And we couldn't afford to get him a real tool kit of his own once everything went bad. He's got a few, but…"

"Tools it is," Matt decided. "And I'd like to get something for Jeff and Hannah. Besides what I'm getting for their wedding," he added. "And something for Dana Brennan and Helen Walker. Helen's always been good to me, and Dana, well…" He paused as though choosing his words, then said, "Dana has treated me kindly through thick and thin. She's one special lady."

"She is." Callie squeezed his hand. "And I'm delighted that Jeff and Hannah are having a New Year's wedding."

Matt bumped her arm. "That we're both attending."

"I—"

"I'll take that as a yes." He grinned, then tugged her along. "Already this is a productive night. I've got a Christmas plan *and* a date for the wedding."

"I didn't say yes," she retorted, shrugging her purse up her other arm. "And you didn't ask. You assumed."

"Will you go with me? Save me from a night of food, romance and music all alone?"

Callie flashed him a once-over. "I don't think you'd be all that lonely."

"Your presence ensures it." He paused outside the cookie and coffee shop. "Want a quick coffee? My treat."

"I'd love one." The piano notes paused as Matt ordered their coffees, then began again, different this time, as though…

Callie jumped as a voice rang out right next to her. Another voice joined in from across the way, followed by two, harmonizing, about eight tables back.

The piano danced along, the flow of voices joined by others as random people stood and sang around the center court.

"A flash mob," Callie breathed, gripping Matt's arm.

He shook his head, not understanding.

"Choral groups and dance troupes put these together and then randomly perform," Callie whispered. She squeezed his arm tighter. "I've always wanted to see one."

"Well, here you go." He smiled down at her as the far-flung choir offered a rousing Christmas medley, their voices blending harmony and praise. As the medley wound down, a lone man mounted a chair in the middle, his haggard appearance making him look cast-out. Wondering. Wandering. Slowly, note by note, he began singing "Joseph's Song," the poignant hymn expressing the awesome wonder and responsibility of guiding God's son through life.

The lone man was singing to him. *Of him,* Matt decided as emotions grabbed hold and refused to let go.

The words filled Matt's heart, easing more of the angst. Simple piano notes balanced the strong tenor of the prayerful man, seeking God's will, a father's advice, wondering where a common man like him fit into such a wondrous plan.

The words, meant for Christ's earthly father, fit any man guiding a child not his own. A part of Matt wished Don had felt this way, that he'd been strong enough to ask God's help and be part of Matt's life.

Another part envisioned Jake, another man's son, a child so sweet, so invested in life that Matt wondered if his presence would bless the boy's life. Could it?

Joseph was a simple carpenter.

Like Matt.

He accepted a child not his own.

A boy, like Jake, to father. Guide. Love. And Joseph embraced his wife despite questionable circumstances. He latched on to faith and clung to an angel's direction.

Could Matt be that strong? Could he embrace Callie and Jake, and be a father in the image of Joseph?

A tiny tear slipped down Callie's cheek, the spiritual words working womanly magic. Matt caught the tear and tugged her closer, holding her. Cherishing her. Wondering what he'd done to have this family put in his path, how this perfect timing had come about. No matter. She was here, and unless he messed up big time, her feelings for him reflected his for her.

Just right.

The song came to a whispered close, the soft chain of notes like a puff of wind.

"Here." Matt handed her a napkin, rolled his eyes and smiled. "Women. Always mushy."

"Like that didn't affect you?" she asked. She poked him with her elbow. "Seriously?"

"Oh, it did." He didn't dare tell her how much.

"But the coffee's getting cold and the mall's open only three more hours."

"Then it's good we've got a short list," she told him.

He smiled and sipped his coffee, thinking the list might grow, whispers of promises and forever afters niggling his brain. But for now, they'd shop. Figure things out. Take this blessed night for what it was: a time to be together. Get to know one another away from the clatter and chatter that surrounded them at work. Tonight they were just a pair of shoppers, out to have a little fun.

He couldn't have asked for more.

Chapter Fourteen

Callie lifted her gaze to survey number thirty-seven's new roofline on Tuesday afternoon and put an arm around her father's waist. "It's beautiful, Dad."

"It is." Hank regarded the black architect shingles, then twisted to eye the homes leading up to this last one. "The neighborhood looks great."

"You do good work for an old soldier," she told him, basking in the gentle day, a rarity for early December. Snow was forecast for tomorrow, so getting these roofs complete, windows in, doors hung was imperative.

The gift of hard work, focus and God's hand with Mother Nature.

"Are you coming to work on the church roof?" Hank asked, rolling his shoulders to ease two straight days of shingling.

Callie shook her head. "You need only a few people. And Jake's bus will be here before the roof's done, so I'm going to finish painting the family room in the model. And the upstairs should be ready for paint soon, leaving us flooring and bathroom tiling to complete things."

"The countertop looks good, Callie," Hank told her as they walked toward Matt's truck. "It has a rich look to it."

"Thanks." She waved toward the model as they drew closer. "The lighter cabinets let me go a little wild with the counter top. You don't think it's too dark?"

Matt came up alongside them, pulling off his hat and gloves. "The lighting offsets the dark tone," he assured her, smiling. "And I think we've had this conversation before."

Callie made a face. "I'm just wondering if that's why those people haven't made an offer, if maybe I messed up the balance and that put them off."

"They said they wanted time to consider their options and pray about it. Stop borrowing trouble." He bumped shoulders with her, then laughed at her scowl. "If they do move in, they'll probably be good neighbors. And with a kid Jake's age, that would be nice. A few days of waiting is worth it to get good neighbors."

"So it's not about the countertop?"

Matt raised his eyes heavenward and climbed into the truck. Hank took his place on the passenger side. "We've got just enough time to get this patched before dark, I think."

Matt nodded agreement, then waved as he backed the truck out of the driveway, the crunch of stones beneath the wheels a temporary sound. By spring

Phase One would be complete, the road and driveways paved. Streetlights would brighten the nights, a torch-lit uphill path complementing the curving road.

They'd have a charming view out the front window, Callie mused as she entered the model. She adjusted the thermostat and smiled, the warmth of the new furnace a welcome presence. Painting a heated family room or working a crisp rooftop? She grinned and shed her gloves, knowing she'd gotten the easy end of this deal.

The front door opened as she rolled paint on the back wall. "Dad? Matt? That you?"

"It's me," said Finch as he strolled through the model, looking left and right, his gaze pinched.

"Hey, Finch." Callie nodded his way and continued working. "Matt's not here, but—"

"I know. That's the reason I came now. To see you."

Callie groaned inside, but kept her face affable. "Really? Why?"

"You and I need to talk," Finch declared. He stood still, folded his arms and braced his legs, battle ready. "It's time you knew a few things about your boss."

Cassie frowned, silent, deliberately obtuse. Rule one of battle: let the enemy state their position.

"You look around here," Finch waved a hand, exasperated, "and you see Matt Cavanaugh as a knight in shining armor. Well, he's not. Not even close."

Callie kept working but flicked a mild look over her shoulder. "Matt took an opportunity that came his way, then stepped in graciously. He's been nothing but a gentleman and a fine contractor. He doesn't cut corners, he doesn't do shoddy and he's generous to a fault."

"Fault is exactly what I'm talking about." Finch encroached on her space, determined and angry. "This guy waltzes into town and you follow him around like a love-struck puppy when you know nothing about him. Who he is, what he's done."

"First of all." Callie set the roller down, pivoted and met Finch's glare with one of her own. "Don't demean me. I'm perfectly capable of making my own decisions in all matters, so I don't need you to save me from myself. I have bills to pay and a child to raise, and working for Matt is a sensible way to do both affordably. Anything else is none of your business. Now if you're not here on town business, please leave."

"I make it town business when I'm keeping my eye on an ex-con."

Her face must have showed a reaction because Finch smirked and came forward again. "You didn't know that, did you? That the guy living in your house, teaching things to your little boy, is an ex-con with a record as long as my arm." He edged close and tsk-tsked her. "You really should pay better attention to who comes through your front door, but then you've always been too trusting."

The best defense is a great offense. Callie strode forward and poked a finger into Finch's very surprised chest. "What is the matter with you, McGee? Why would you come in here trying to stir up trouble? You think I don't know Matt had problems?" She raised her voice and stood tall, straight and taut, a soldier's stance.

"When I was a child, I talked as a child," she summarized the wise verse from Corinthians. "And when I became a man I gave up childish ways." She leaned in, refusing to give ground, determined to have this out with Finch once and for all, hoping it wouldn't affect Matt's certificates of occupancy. "Everybody makes mistakes when they're kids, Finch, and sometimes when they're not kids. But grown-ups move forward and fix things. Do the right thing. So Matt made mistakes. Well, me, too. And I don't think that mirror you face every morning shows a man without scars, so how about we turn this around and figure out why you've been a jerk for two years."

Finch paled, but didn't back down.

"Your marriage failed. And I don't know anything about it, but I bet there's plenty of blame to go around. And you're mad at the world. That two-by-four chip on your shoulder's gotta feel pretty heavy by the end of the day, so why don't you wise up, take your troubles to God, go to church and make things right," Callie halved the narrow distance between 'em and tightened her gaze, "because I don't want some showing up here angry anymore unless there's Matt ag" ing on site to be angry about. If you lay into in any way, about his work methods, or malign him personal issues to have them put Colby in your place."

"You wouldn't."

"Would."

"But—"

"There are no buts," Callie told him. She squared her shoulders. "Stop living in the past, stop making trouble and do your job. I don't care what Matt Cavanaugh did before, what I care about is the future. And right now, Matt's work is the cornerstone of success for Cobbled Creek, and if you continue to try and thwart that, I'll…"

"I get it."

"Good." She nailed him with a glare, then sighed. "Finch, I don't pretend to understand what's going on with you, but you didn't used to be like this. Get a grip. Stop drinking, stop whining and move on."

Finch stared beyond her for a long moment, then shifted his attention back. "I've tried. Or thought I did. First it was Katie, way back when, but she didn't have eyes for anyone but Matt. Even after he crashed that car and crippled her, she longed for him. Talked about him. Wanted to help him, when all I wanted was a piece of him for being so stupid."

Matt had been driving the car the night of Katie's accident. Callie sighed inside, understanding how old wrongs could burn a hole deep into your soul. But only if you allowed it to happen. She swallowed hard, recognizing her own struggles, and couldn't help but wonder if two people with so many doubts could possibly be good for one another. But for now, she needed to set things straight with Finch.

"So this is about a two-decades-old romance gone

bad?" Callie folded her arms and sighed. "Get over it already."

"And then there was you," Finch went on. "You knew I was interested."

"But I wasn't," Callie declared because her more subtle clues hadn't worked.

"I got that when I saw you get all goofy about Cavanaugh the first time I came by," Finch told her. "But then I saw him out with Katie and I wanted to punch someone."

"But you didn't." Callie sent him a look of sympathy. "That was good."

He growled and scrubbed a toe against the subflooring. "I miss my wife. I messed up big time. Not being home, being on time, helping with things, going to kid stuff. I got careless and she walked." He lifted his gaze to Callie's. "And now she's in Arizona with my kids, dating a land developer, and then Cavanaugh shows up here, playing the hero…"

Callie recognized the parallel. "You had a lot of buttons being pushed, Finch, but that wasn't Matt's fault."

"Katie's missing leg is Matt's fault," Finch declared, brows drawn. Then he sighed and acknowledged, "But that was twenty years ago."

"And she's obviously forgiven him," Callie added, remembering the picture.

"She never blamed him."

Callie could understand that. Katie's gentle nature reached out to others, nothing like her hypercritical father. "Katie's a sweetheart."

"She is."

"But Finch," Callie went on, determined to make her point. "You've got to stop spinning your wheels thinking you can determine the next steps. Let go and let God."

He grunted.

"I'm serious," Callie continued. "You said your marriage failed because you stopped paying attention to little things. I disagree. It failed because you missed the boat on one big thing: faith. If you'd grounded yourself in God's love, you wouldn't have messed up in the first place."

"You sound like my mother."

Callie grinned. "Your mother is a smart woman. Finch, you can fix this." She reached out a hand to his arm. "But there are no shortcuts, no quick inroads. And you shouldn't be concerning yourself with romance until you're on solid ground again. Restructure your priorities. God. Family. Country. Friends. And no more beer."

He hauled in a deep breath and exhaled slowly. "Is there a charge for this therapy session?"

Callie smiled and chucked him on the arm. "There will be if the paint on my roller gets tacky and I have to change it. That baby cost two-nineteen in the contractor's pack."

Finch flashed a sheepish grin as Callie picked up the roller. "Nothing but the best."

"Exactly." Callie tested the nubby surface and nodded, satisfied. "I'm glad you stopped by, Finch."

He made a face of disbelief. Callie caught it and

smiled. "I mean it. It's better to clear the air than go on dodging bullets. And if you need help…"

"More therapy?"

"Exactly." She nodded, empathetic. "I've gone down your road. I had a husband walk out on me, so I know it's a tough go, but faith and family can get you through anything. But I'd be glad to talk to you more. As friends," she added, sending him a pointed look of amusement over her shoulder.

"Got it." He started to leave, then turned back. "Thanks, Callie. I hope Cavanaugh knows how lucky he is."

"He does," said Matt as he entered from the garage, his eyes sweeping the scene, his expression battlefield ready.

"Everything looks good," Finch told him, waving a hand.

Matt paused, weighing the words. "No problems?"

Finch sent a look of gratitude toward Callie. "None we haven't solved. Thanks again, Callie. I'll be back to check the electric and plumbing lines on the other houses whenever they're ready, Matt."

"I'll call."

"And don't worry about that two-day stuff either."

"You don't need quite that much time?" Matt asked. Callie kept working, but felt his gaze sweep her and Finch again.

"Work's slow," Finch admitted in a tone of voice that sounded like the guy she'd known years before. "Call anytime. I might even be able to come right out."

Matt smiled. "Thanks. Time's tight now with the weather and all."

"And time's money," Finch added. He nodded and headed for the door. "See you Sunday, Callie. If not before."

She smiled, satisfied. "Looking forward to it, Finch."

Matt was pretty certain he'd walked into an alternate universe.

Callie frowned up at him as she refilled her roller. "Why aren't you roofing at the church?"

"Buck, Jim and your dad have it under control, so I thought I'd come back here and help you." He moved closer and nodded approval, the new paint brightening the south-facing room. "This is beautiful, Cal."

"Isn't it?" She flashed him a smile that brightened the room even more. "I thought it might be too yellow, but it's not. It's just soft enough to reflect the light and keep things warm. Appealing."

"I agree," he said, but he aimed his look at her, not the wall.

"Matt."

"Callie." He moved forward and took the roller out of her hands, wondering when the smell of new paint became so wonderfully enticing. Or maybe it was the smudge on her cheek, the tiny roller spatters across her nose? He rubbed a gentle finger to make them disappear, and sighed, the feel of being close to her a new experience, sweet and good. Inviting. "You smell good."

She grinned and daubed a tiny bit of paint to his face with her finger. "I smell like paint."

He gave her a lazy smile and tightened his grip. "Then I must really like paint, because..." he let his kiss fill in the blank, the combination of Callie, fresh-sawn wood and new paint bringing all the factors of his world together in one pleasurable experience. He had no idea how long the kiss lasted, and really didn't care because he'd like for it to never end, but the rumble of the school bus engine interrupted way too soon. "Jake's home."

"Uh-huh."

He grinned down at her, glad he had a few inches on her in her work shoes, a height advantage that disappeared when she wore heels.

He didn't care. Tall, short, thin, wide, messy or dressed up, to him she was just Callie, the most delightful creature God could have put in his path. As the bus brakes squealed to a stop, he drew her forward. "Let's go meet the kid. I've got a surprise for us."

"A surprise?"

He smiled, set her roller down, then ushered her out the door.

The quick drop in temperature made the forecasted snow seem more real. Callie tugged her flannel tighter as she and Matt waited. Jake raced to see them, excitement showing in every step. "Hey, I got another A on my math paper, Mom!"

"Wonderful!" Callie high-fived him, then stepped

back inside the warm house. "Seriously, Matt? It's freezing out there."

Matt and Jake followed her inside and Matt shut the door. "I know, it started dropping about the time we got on that roof."

"So we're patching it just in time," Callie noted.

"Yes." Matt ruffled Jake's hair and added, "Looks like snow tomorrow. And from then on, who knows?"

"I love snow!"

"Most kids do," Matt told him. He reached into his back pocket and held up a flat rectangular piece of card stock. "And once it snows, we're taking a sleigh ride. If that's okay?" he asked Callie, raising his gaze to her as Jake attacked his legs.

"Matt, you shouldn't have…"

"Sure he should," Jake told her, astonished. "Because he knew I wanted to go and it's cheaper if three go, right? Because then we can each pay a third."

"Well, that's a mighty generous offer, bud," Matt drawled, making sure graciousness hid the laughter in his tone. "But I've got this one covered. Kind of a thank-you to you and your mom for all the hard work you do over here."

"But isn't that why you pay us?" Jake wondered out loud. "That's what Mom says anyway. You work hard and get paid for the work you do. She didn't say anything about a sleigh ride in the park with the lights."

"That's a fringe benefit, Jake," Matt explained, exchanging smiles with Callie. "When you work really hard, sometimes extra benefits go with the job."

His words drove up the heat in Callie's cheeks, and that delighted him.

"Then I like those fringe benefit things," Jake declared.

Matt sent a teasing look to Jake's mother. "Me, too."

"And on that note..." Callie headed back to the family room. "I need to get this finished. And our fire is probably out at home, so can you guys start one? And let The General out for a run?"

"Will do."

Jake headed out, but Matt lingered. "So, Finch's visit..." he trailed the words, an eyebrow arched.

"Something we'll talk about without little ears around," Callie told him.

Matt weighed the words and her expression. "He told you about my past."

"Yes. And I reminded him," Callie kept her voice even as she rolled the wall, "that everybody makes mistakes. And nothing's unfixable."

Matt clenched his hands, wishing that was true.

"Even Katie's leg," Callie went on. She met his gaze across the room and noted his hands with a glance. "We move on. We try harder. Stay strong. Everyone has a past, Matt."

"Even you?"

Her flush said yes. Her eyes said it wasn't a topic she was ready to explore which meant she'd buried the hurt, just like him. That only made him more determined to fix it. "Don't you have a fire to start?"

"I'm on it."

"Good. And Matt?"

He turned, the sound of her voice a sweeter draw than wood fire flames on a dark December night. "Yes?"

"Thank you."

"For?" He frowned, not understanding, then nodded and raised the ticket. "Oh. Of course. You're welcome."

Callie shook her head and met his look across the room, then waved a hand indicating the house, the road, the subdivision. Herself. "For all of it. Thank you."

He loved her. He knew it fully and truly, standing there, seeing her decked out in spattered work clothes, a day's labor behind her and still ready to do whatever it took to be a good mother. A fine daughter. And maybe, just maybe, something more.

He sighed, smiled and nodded, wishing he could kick his heels in the air like Jake and the pooch. "You're welcome, Cal."

He headed across the field, whistling the "Marine's Hymn," keeping pace with the rhythm and the beat, his soul blessed, his heart... Well, full was the best way to describe that, and while it was an unfamiliar feeling, Matt decided he liked it. A lot.

He eyed the Quiltin' Bee as he passed through Jamison a couple of hours later, then parked the truck and headed inside, determined to make sure Callie had a great Christmas. He waited while Maude finished up with a customer, then frowned when she reached beneath the counter and withdrew a festively-wrapped box topped by a big red bow.

"This is?"

"Callie's quilt." She handed him a bill and added, "And if you don't have the money now, I'll wait."

"I've got it," Matt told her as he withdrew his wallet. "What I'm wondering is how you knew I'd be back."

She sent him a wizened grin. "At my age, there's less I don't know than I do. One look at you and Callie on the park round, well…" She softened the smile and shrugged. "Things just seemed to fit."

Matt couldn't disagree. He handed her his debit card, signed his name, then tucked the box carefully behind the seat of his truck, feeling like he was truly getting ready for the old-fashioned Christmas he'd dreamed of as a kid.

Chapter Fifteen

Callie watched Matt tuck the lap robe snug around Jake's legs a few nights later and tumbled right back into the danger zone she'd pledged to avoid. Matt's grin and Jake's answering broad smile made it seem less dangerous and more charming.

Matt climbed into the sleigh, slipped an arm around her shoulders and dropped a kiss to her hair.

If she hadn't tilted head over heels before, she did then, the feel of a strong, rugged marine taking charge, leading in ways of goodness and grace, here with her and Jake, fulfilling a little boy's dream. And maybe a big boy's as well, if the look on his face was any indication. She leaned closer. "I'm not sure which one of you is smiling more," she noted as they passed beneath a lighted arch made of naturally entwined tree branches and thousands of tiny twinkle lights.

"This is amazing."

"It is." Jake grinned up at Matt, his joy palpable. He wriggled beneath the blanket as they came upon an action scene of animatronic elves in Santa's workshop. "Mom, look! They're building a tool bench!"

Callie laughed out loud. "Those are my kind of elves, Jake. And see what Mrs. Santa's doing?" She pointed toward the left of the scene, where Mrs. Santa and a couple of girl elves fashioned baby dolls. "So sweet."

Jake snorted. "They're dolls."

Matt gave Callie's arm a gentle squeeze. "Did you like playing with dolls when you were little or were you always a tomboy?"

"Both," she told him, smiling. "I was never afraid to get dirty or run with the boys and play sports, but…" she slanted him a teasing look, "even then I cleaned up well."

He hugged her shoulder tighter, laughing. "Some things never change. Hey, do you see those reindeer?"

"A real Santa scene," breathed Jake as they drew closer, the horse hooves clip-clopping along the curved road. A well-dressed robust Santa groomed a small herd of reindeer, on loan from a local organic farm, and the picture added a dose of reality to the fantasyland surrounding them.

"Nice," Matt observed, his gaze roaming as if hungering for the next sight, the coming scene. They passed through a tree-lined path bathed in white twinkle lights, a Currier and Ives setting with the sleigh, the horse, the driver, the trees. A photographer snapped their photo as they emerged from the boughs, and Callie wondered if the photo would capture how perfect the moment felt.

Lighted scenes peppered the woods on both sides

until they turned a corner that led them into the midst of a living nativity, spot-lit from all angles. Mary and Joseph hovered over a hay-filled manger, concern painting their features, while shepherds gathered in awe, chatting and exclaiming.

Sheep wandered the area, their thick woolly coats dusted with snow. A donkey stood to the right, placidly munching hay. Two well-dressed angels watched over the scene from above, their raised platforms hidden by dark draperies, while two more knelt below, paying homage to a newborn king, a child of the poor.

"Oh, Matt." Jake clenched Matt's arm and the sincerity in his young voice had Callie fighting tears. "They did it just right," Jake continued, awestruck. "The wise men aren't here, but the angels are gathering around. And the shepherds came back to see if the angels were right. And they were."

"Of course they were," Matt assured him.

Did his voice break a little? Callie peeked up, and the loving expression on his face made suppressing an overload of emotions impossible.

"Whenever I think of what Jesus did for us, I regret every time I whine or crab about anything. Born in a manger, hung on a cross." Matt shook his head and sighed. "And when I feel the most unworthy, I remember he did it for the least of us. And then I feel better."

Jake reached over Callie and hugged Matt. "I love you, Matt."

Fear and hope mixed like concrete and stone in

Callie's gut. The thought of how bad this could be began to rise up, but then Jake leaned back and stared up into Matt's face. "If I had a dad, I'd want him to be like you. You're nice to kids like me and that's a good thing for a dad to do."

The look of love Matt settled on the boy was enhanced by the big, broad hand he laid against Jake's cheek. "You're right, bud. That's exactly what dads should do."

Jake matched and met Matt's smile, then sat back. "This is the most beautiful night I ever had."

Matt heard the boy's words and glimpsed Callie's tear-streaked face and realized he was in for the long haul. Only a rotter would back out now, and Matt had no intention of backing away from this family.

Callie fumbled for a tissue, wiped her eyes and blew her nose, then mock-scowled at him for sending a laughing glance her way. "It's cold out here."

"Uh-huh." He leaned closer, his mouth to her ear. "I think you're a sap, soldier. But pretty enough to be kissed." And he did that, right there, a sweet, gentle kiss feathering over her face, her mouth, not caring if Jake saw because Matt had every intention of establishing his very own family in Cobbled Creek.

If she'd have him, of course. But from the look on her face Matt was pretty sure nothing could get in their way.

"Hey, Matt. What's up?" Jeff Brennan pulled up next to Matt's car at a Wellsville gas station the next afternoon. "I keep meaning to get over to Cobbled Creek, but the factory's crazy busy. How are things going? Okay?"

Matt turned and shot a smile toward his half brother. *Brother,* he corrected himself, determined to mend every relationship he could, regardless of legality.

He nodded. "Amazing, actually. And you were right when you told me the Mareks are wonderful people. And I've got my stepdad doing drywall for me."

He hesitated saying that last bit, pretty sure Jeff would think it weird. As if their convoluted relationships could get any stranger than they already were.

"Awkward." Jeff sent Matt a look of understanding. "But because that describes our family to a tee, it's a good place to start over."

"He's sick, too."

"Yeah?" Jeff's sympathetic expression said he empathized. "What's his prognosis?"

"Good. Just a road to travel. A rough go, alone."

"So it's nice he has you."

"I guess." At this moment Matt wasn't too sure what purpose he served anywhere, except with a hammer in his hands. Give him a toolbox and suddenly everything made sense. "Everybody's gotta have someone, right? How are the wedding plans coming?"

Jeff grinned. "Hannah and I put them in Mom's capable hands. She's happy, she's got Meredith to help her, and we're delighted to let things happen around us."

"Your mother's great," Matt told him. Jeff's mother had been the only person other than Grandpa Gus to visit Matt in juvie, and that was after Dana Brennan had her private life gossiped about in every home when the world discovered Matt was her husband's illegitimate son.

"She is. And you're coming over for Christmas, right?"

"Well…"

"Like you've got a better offer?" Jeff's teasing tone said he doubted that.

"I…um…"

"You *do* have a better offer," Jeff mused. His left eyebrow shifted up. "Which means the Marek family, because you've been holed up in Cobbled Creek for weeks."

"I might be spending it with them. Yes."

"With Callie, you mean."

Matt was hoping for that very thing, but… "Keep a spot at the table open for me. Just in case."

Jeff gave him a brotherly arm punch. "Will do. Although Mom likes nothing more than planning special events. So she'd be glad to jump in and help with anything you might need. You know that, don't you?"

Maybe he'd said too much. Or at least too soon. Matt leaned down. "Hey, about Christmas and the Mareks, don't say anything, okay?"

Jeff's grin spread wide. "You'll owe me."

Maybe having a brother wasn't such a great thing after all. "For?"

"Buying my silence."

Matt thought of how convoluted his life had just become and didn't hold back his sigh. "This one time, it will be worth it."

Jeff laughed and drove off, leaving Matt feeling like life was racing forward at break-neck speed and he'd forgotten how to apply the brakes. Except he didn't want to, not really. And he was surprised at how good that felt.

She should stay home, Callie decided, eyeing the storm and the clock on Saturday afternoon.

She moved toward the phone, then paused and studied her hands, strong and blunt. Weathered. Tough.

She should be working. Helping. The guys had been at it all day, with her at their side, until she took Jake to Cole's house to play.

And that was the difference, she realized. Jake was a little boy. Playtime was important for his growth and development. Hers?

Not so much.

She reached for the phone, but paused again, wondering. Was it so bad to take a little time for herself? Do something frivolous?

Not to mention pricey. With money scarce, why would she even consider seeing Matt's sister about something as useless as a manicure?

Hannah's arrival nixed the cancellation call. She

grinned as Callie climbed in the passenger seat, then laughed at the look Callie shot her.

"Cal, seriously, it's not a firing squad. It's a manicure. And it's Meredith. We'll have a great time."

Callie indicated Cobbled Creek with a thrust of her jaw. "Do you know how many things I should be doing right now?"

Hannah laid a hand atop Callie's. "Listen, Martha…"

Callie smiled and groaned, the biblical analogy clear. Martha was the energetic, hardworking, get-'er-done sister of Lazarus. Mary was the quiet listener at God's feet.

"Every now and again, it's okay to take a little time off. Have some fun. And there's nothing wrong with taking care of yourself."

They pulled up to Dana Brennan's beautiful home, sprawling on a double village lot, a detached carriage house-style garage around the back. Callie sighed. "This is gorgeous."

"Isn't it?" Hannah headed for the side entrance. She pushed open the door, waved hello and turned back. "Callie, you remember Meredith, don't you?"

"I do."

One look at Meredith's flawless beauty, her stylish outfit, and Callie wished she'd opted out.

"Although high school was a long time ago." Callie reached out a hand, trying not to bumble, wondering if she should make a run for the door. "I was a year behind you."

"Callie." Meredith grabbed Callie's hands and

drew her in, her smile infectious. "I'm so glad you came over. Hannah said Matt's been working you night and day, and you need a little pampering."

"No, oh, no." Callie shook her head in quick denial. She darted a troubled look at Hannah. "Matt wouldn't think of such a thing, I mean, he's always after me to slow down. Take time off. Relax a little."

Meredith shot Hannah a quick, knowing glance. "Whoa, spot-on. She's got it bad."

"Told ya."

"Hey." Callie frowned Hannah's way, but Hannah moved across the spacious kitchen, ignoring her.

"Come in here." Meredith tugged her forward, laughing, a feminine version of Matt's laugh. Warm. Enticing. Vibrant. "I was only kidding, but you totally took the bait, so there's no denying the spark going on between you and my brother."

"We work together," Callie insisted.

"Oh, we get it, honey." Hannah set out a box of fresh brownies. "I got these in case we needed to bribe you to talk, but as you can see," she waved a hand toward Callie but eyed Meredith, "Totally unnecessary."

"Which means we can probe her for further information about Matt."

"All the good stuff." Hannah withdrew a brownie, grinning.

"Every little detail." Meredith half sang the words in anticipation.

Callie burst out laughing. "Stop. Both of you. I'm

not saying a thing. He'd be mortified to think we're talking about him like this."

"More like complimented beyond belief," Meredith argued in sister-like fashion. "But we'll shelve that for later." She took a seat alongside Callie and seized her hands, her fingers and eyes examining Callie's roughed-up skin. Seeing her hands against Meredith's more feminine version made Callie want to shrink back. Maybe run for her life, but then Meredith met Callie's eyes. "You wondered if I could help you, right?"

Self-conscious, Callie fidgeted. "Yes."

"Oh, honey." Meredith squeezed Callie's hands but leaned in, smiling. "I can work wonders on the skin and the nails, but what you've got here," she raised Callie's hands slightly, "are the hands of a woman unafraid to get the job done. And no matter what you might think up here," Meredith tapped her head with one tapered, manicured finger, "God has blessed you with beautiful hands to match a wonderful heart. I can create pretty-looking skin." She met Callie's look with a bright, knowing smile. "But only God can create amazing hands like yours."

"I—" Callie sat back, touched, pleased and not a little embarrassed.

"Having said that," Meredith grinned, stood, crossed the room and wheeled back a manicure tray, "let's have a little fun, shall we, girls?" She bent and plugged in a cord, then immersed Callie's hands in the small sink.

Jets of warm water soothed Callie's skin. Her hand muscles. Her fingertips, alternately chilled and dried by nature and job conditions. And as Meredith went through her usual routine of soaking, massaging, oiling and waxing, Callie's heart began to relax along with her skin. By the time Meredith put a finishing coat of clear polish on Callie's French manicure, Callie's hands felt nurtured. Cared for. Pampered.

Not that she'd be able to grow accustomed to this, but for once, to feel soft, feminine hands? Smooth-as-silk skin?

Delightful.

And by the time Meredith finished pampering her, Callie felt like she'd known the other woman forever. Meredith wasn't anything like Callie remembered from high school, but then, neither was she.

"Thank you." She reached out and gave Meredith a hug while Hannah gathered their scarves and gloves. "They feel wonderful."

"Aw, you're welcome." And when Callie tried to hand Meredith money, the other woman waved it off, smiling. "Family gets free perks."

"But I'm not family."

Meredith and Hannah exchanged smiles. "A simple matter of timing, honey." Meredith grinned at Callie's bemused expression and high-fived Hannah. "And having another girl around…"

"One who knows how to get things done," Hannah interjected.

"And puts a smile on Matt's face," Meredith added. "That's like the best Christmas present ever, right there."

Callie fought down the blush Meredith's words inspired, but felt the truth of them in her heart. Her soul.

Matt did like being with her. And seeing his sisters' joint approval?

That just made a season of miracles seem more possible than she'd ever considered before.

Five o'clock.

He was late and in danger of missing Jake's part in the Christmas Salute to Veterans concert at the elementary school, Matt realized as darkness fell that evening.

He finalized the wallboard contract for the remaining houses, rushed back to the Mareks' and jumped into uniform, wishing he'd had someone else swing south to pick up Don. Matt headed down Route 19 and turned west toward Don's apartment, impatient. He parked in the only available spot half-a-block down and dashed for Don's house, wishing he'd paid closer attention to the time.

Don's porch light clicked on. He pulled open the inner door, pivoted to shut it, then turned and stopped, staring at Matt as though he'd never seen him before.

The uniform, Matt realized.

"Ready?"

Don nodded. His gaze flicked up and down, then up again. "You look great."

"Well, thanks." Matt wore the formal uniform with pride, but he hadn't pulled it out since a funeral the previous year. He'd forgotten the reaction it drew from people. Don's was classic. "Sorry I'm late. Think we'll make it in time?"

Don put a hand to his arm, his expression tight. "I'm proud of you, Matt."

Part of Matt's heart churned. He'd have loved to hear those words twenty-five years ago. Now? Discomfort crept up his spine.

Now he just needed to get to Jake's concert in time to see the boy sing. He shrugged, embarrassed. "Let's go."

The overflowing parking lot said they'd gotten there far too late to find Callie and Hank in the uniform-studded audience.

She found them instead, and that made Matt feel special. Beloved. Her waving hand beckoned from down front. He let Don precede him and followed, drawn by a sweet force that linked him to her. "Hey." He flashed a quick smile, grateful. "You saved us seats?"

"Yes."

"Thanks, Cal."

"You're looking good, marine."

He duffed the collar of her desert camo. "You, too."

She made a little face of disbelief, but Matt tucked a finger beneath her chin until she met his gaze. "You're absolutely beautiful, Cal. No matter what you're wearing."

Her eyes searched his, questioning. Wondering. He hoped his sincerity and intent showed in his answering look. Something must have telegraphed through because she ducked, blushing.

The blush. The smile. The averted gaze…

They had it bad, Matt realized anew. And he'd never imagined that having it bad could be so wonderfully good. But it was, right down to planning a future he'd refused to ponder, but being with Callie? Loving her?

Anything seemed possible.

He sat beside her, her soft fingers clasped in his, ready to lay old doubts at God's feet, determined to grasp the life God offered, sweet and fulfilling. A life he didn't think he deserved, but he was finally learning not to question God's judgment.

Or Callie's embracing smile.

Maybe, just maybe, he could have it all.

Chapter Sixteen

Callie saw the message light flashing on the home phone as she made coffee for the crew on Monday afternoon, sweet memories of Jake's concert, Matt's presence and Christmas brightening the day. She listened to Mary Kay's excited news, then left the coffee to drip while she drove over to the subdivision. She burst into number seventeen, skirted an electrician running wire and cornered Matt in the great room. "They put an offer in on number twenty-three!"

Matt's brows shot up. "Really? How do you know this?"

"Your cell must be down. Mary Kay left a message on the home phone."

Matt grabbed her, spun her around and then just held her, the steady beat of his heart like music to her ears. "This is wonderful," he whispered.

"Yes." Oh, it was. To be held like this? Respected? Beyond wonderful.

"Good news?" Hank asked from above.

Matt fist pumped the air with one hand. "We've got our first sale."

Hank grinned and let his gaze linger on them. "Among other things."

Callie sidestepped Matt's arm. "Just celebrating success, Dad."

"We should do a special dinner tonight," Matt announced.

"As in?"

"We'll go to The Edge. Celebrate. The whole crew." The Edge was the area's acclaimed fine-dining experience.

Hank leaned over the roughed-in stairway. "Well, that gets mighty pricey. Let's save that meal for when we've got all nine sold. How 'bout for tonight we just throw some good steaks on the grill? It's snowing, but I don't mind cookin' in the snow."

"And we'll make baked potatoes," Callie offered.

"And cauliflower with cheese sauce," added Tom from a room away. "And rolls from the bakery."

"Then we need to shop." Callie glanced at her watch and frowned. Jake's bus would be along soon, but she hated to miss work time for errands.

"I've got to grab some things in town once I'm finished here," Matt told them. "I'll pick up the steaks, cauliflower and rolls."

"Excellent."

His grin reflected her feelings. It was good to have that first house sold, a done deal, long-awaited. "I ran over here to tell you before the coffee finished up, so when I'm back at the house I'm doing two things,"

Callie told him. "I'm calling to order the steaks because they might not have enough nice ones in the case this late in the day."

"Good idea."

"And I'm ordering a landline phone for the model," Callie continued. "And setting up a spare coffeepot there. It's silly to run across the road for coffee now."

"Go for it." He sent her a smile that made her heart feel like they were a team. "And don't bring coffee back for me. I'm going to finish this piece and get the errands done so we don't eat too late for Jake to enjoy it."

"As long as it includes ice cream, Jake'll love it," Hank told him. The smile of satisfaction lighting his face made Callie realize she hadn't seen her father look this at ease in years.

Darkness had descended by the time they'd washed up and gathered at the Marek house. Callie and Jake filled a big bowl with bright red punch, and as each man lumbered into the kitchen, Jake served him a fancy tiny-handled cup of the special concoction.

And not one of those big, burly guys laughed at the prissy glass cup they held.

Matt gave a short, sharp whistle. Conversation stopped as everyone turned his way. He raised his punch cup and surveyed the room, the glimmer of Christmas lights backlighting him. "Since none of us want those steaks to burn, I just want to thank all of you. To Hank and Callie," he met Hank's smile and matched it. "For your initial vision and hard work.

And letting me bunk here. That proximity means the world to me." He smiled again and Callie hoped he meant proximity to more than the half-built houses.

"Buck, Tom, Jim and Amanda." He nodded to that group. "None of this would have been possible without you guys. You know that, don't you?"

They hemmed and hawed, embarrassed.

"And to Don." Matt turned to his stepfather deliberately and lofted the cup a little higher. "I've never seen better workmanship in drywall and that perfect finishing touch polishes the entire effect. Thank you. It's nice having family on board."

Don's face paled. His hand shook. He opened his mouth to say something, then paused, overcome, unable to speak. Amanda swiped a quick hand to her face when Matt and Don exchanged looks of understanding.

Matt veered his attention to Jake. "And to you, my young friend. I don't think there's ever been a better apprentice in this business and I mean that. Good job, bud."

Jake manned his glass cup of punch with all the seriousness an eight-year-old could muster. "Thanks, Matt."

"To us." Matt raised his cup higher. "To our continued good work and success. And let's not forget to thank God for that stretch of good weather, because—" Matt deadpanned a look outdoors, "—I think it was slated to be our last."

They sipped in unison, and Callie marveled at how quickly things had turned around. Six weeks before they'd been watching Cobbled Creek fade before their eyes. The view from her front window now embraced a lovely neighborhood, the hopes and dreams of two families coming together.

Matt gave Jake a quick hug and settled on the floor with him to play a quick round of checkers before dinner. Amanda came into the kitchen to help Callie. She swept Matt and Jake a smiling look. "Pretty nice scene, Cal."

"It is."

"The kind a girl could get used to," Amanda added.

"If the girl were one of those romance-loving gals who believed in happily ever afters," Callie replied, although when she was around Matt Cavanaugh it was easier to dream. Hope. Believe.

"And that's the nice thing about life." Amanda trailed the words, her eyes laughing at Callie's attempt to maintain distance. "Things have a way of changing up when you least expect it."

"Steaks are done," Hank called out as he came back inside.

"Great." Matt stood, pulled Jake up beside him and surveyed the laden table, gratitude marking his expression. "Thanks for doing this, Callie, because you prefer a hammer to a stovetop."

"You know I make exceptions now and again." She sent him a smile across the table, and hoped he read the pride she felt. Working for him, seeing the homes progress, watching this plan come together at long last.

"I'm glad," Matt told her. His tone said he read her expression correctly.

Jake sat at a card table they set up in the living room with the two Slaughter kids. Once Amanda had them settled, the crew gathered around the table, the mixed scents of rich meat, tangy cheese and fresh-baked rolls teasing the senses. "God, you've blessed us with Matt Cavanaugh," Hank intoned as they clasped hands around the table. "You brought him to us and gathered us together. We thank you for that, and this food. Amen."

"Amen."

"Short and sweet." Buck nodded, affable. "Good job."

"Can't let the meat get cold," said Hank. "And I don't want this to go to Matt's head. All this thankin' business."

"Wouldn't want that." Matt grinned at him, and took a bite of steak. "And right now I can tell you that no one on this planet cooks a better steak than you, Hank."

"Timing." Hank smiled as he savored his own first bite, but he let his eyes twinkle Matt's way. "It's all in the timing, son."

Matt read Hank's look and recognized the truth in the words. He turned toward Don. "Did I hear you say you've got a doctor's appointment tomorrow afternoon?"

"Yes."

"I'll go along."

Don started to shake his head, obviously uncomfortable, but Matt put him off. "No sense arguing. I know it's at the cancer clinic and that these guys all know about it, so we'll stop work around two and head over there, okay?"

Don's nod said he didn't trust himself to speak.

"And Matt," Buck cut in, jutting his chin toward the subdivision, "I'm putting the plow on my truck tomorrow so I'll keep the roadway into the houses cleaned out for us, okay?"

"Buck, that would be awesome. Thank you."

Buck shrugged that off. "Not too many weeks ago this was stretching to be a long, bad winter." He sipped from his tiny, glass cup and grinned at the looks the other guys shot him. "But now? Well, now," he raised his cup high in salute to Matt, the Mareks and Cobbled Creek, "things are looking up."

Hank had thanked God for him, Matt mused as he and Don headed toward the clinic in Wellsville the following afternoon. The idea that anyone placed stock in him both pleased and scared Matt, but with the Marek family? He'd go with mostly pleased.

He pulled up to the clinic's door, dropped Don off and proceeded to an open parking space at the back of the snowy lot. As he pushed through the entrance door, he spotted Don being led to a treatment room down a back corridor. Matt settled into an empty seat, picked up a sports magazine and started rifling the pages.

"Burdick? Joyce Burdick?"

"Here." An older woman stood slowly, a haze of pain creasing her features.

"Lean on me, Mom."

The older woman sent her son a fond look. "It's nice to have you home this weekend, Dustin."

"It's good to be here."

Dustin Burdick. Callie's ex-husband. Jake's dad. He was in town, but hadn't told Callie or asked to see his son.

Matt felt like he'd been punched in the gut. He had to hold himself back from having it out with the guy then and there.

"The treatment will take about an hour once we get her settled in," explained the nurse as an orderly helped Dustin's mother into a wheelchair. "So if you want to come back in about ninety minutes, that would be fine."

"Thanks." Dustin bent and kissed his mother's cheek, then headed for the door. "I'll get that Christmas stuff for you, Mom."

"Thanks, honey."

Honey?

The sweet endearment might mean something coming from Dustin Burdick's mother, but Matt found the irony too much to bear. He followed Dustin outside and called his name. Dustin turned, surprise and caution vying for his features. "Yes?"

"You're in town for the weekend?"

Dustin shifted left. "Do I know you?"

"No." Matt braced his feet and folded his arms, keeping his voice and expression taut. "But I know your ex-wife. And your son. And I'm just wondering what kind of guy walks out on a great kid like Jake and never calls. Never sends cards or gifts. Never visits his own flesh and blood. What kind of soldier were you when you can treat your own family like that?"

"Who are you? And what business is it of yours?" Dustin growled the words, his displeasure apparent.

"Callie works for me." *Lame, Cavanaugh, when Callie was so much more than an employee.* Still, he wasn't about to share their relationship with Dustin Burdick, a cheating spouse and deadbeat father. Matt had enough of that to last a lifetime. "And you didn't answer the question. How can you walk out on a kid like that? Just turn your back and go?"

Matt didn't try to fool himself that cornering Dustin in a public parking lot was the smartest thing he'd ever done, but good marines seize opportunities God sends their way. And today God put Dustin square in Matt's path.

Dustin sent him a cool look of appraisal. "I don't know who you are or what it matters to you, but I don't have to answer to anyone. I have a life. Callie has a life. We've both moved on. I suggest you do the same."

"You moved on while you were married to her." Matt kept his voice intentionally soft on purpose. More threatening that way. "You cheated on her, then walked out on your wife and infant son. You discredit the uniform."

Dustin took a step forward and hooked a thumb

toward himself. "I hated the uniform. The rules. The time. The drills. The waiting around in hundred-and-ten-degree weather, half hoping something would happen. And there was Callie, kind of cute, working on the base. I'd known her in high school, so when we met up in Iraq…" He shrugged, nonchalant. "It gave me something to do."

Anger put a chokehold on Matt. Dustin married Callie for something to do?

The temptation to beat the stuffing out of this guy forced Matt back. He held up a hand. "You're not interested in being Jake's father? His dad?"

Dustin scowled. "I've got two kids. I'm lucky I can afford them. And don't have Callie try to garnish my wages again either. You can't take blood from a stone and she'll get nothing."

Matt appraised Dustin's leather coat and upscale jeans. "You hide your income so you don't have to support Jake."

Dustin's face said "Yes" as he shook his head. "I've got no income. Fresh out."

A flash of inspiration hit Matt, a possible way to emerge a winner from a bad confrontation. "Will you give up your rights to Jake?"

Dustin's scowl deepened. "Where do I sign?"

Matt really wanted to punch this guy. His fingers ached for wanting. But more than that, he wanted to be free to make Jake his own. If Callie would have him, that is. "If I have the papers sent to you, will you sign off as Jake's dad?"

"I don't have to worry about anybody coming after me for money ever again?"

No, dirtbag. Matt kept that feeling to himself, but it took effort. What he said out loud was, "Exactly. You'll be free and clear and I can adopt Jake."

A light sparked in Dustin's eyes. "This might be worth something to you, then?"

Matt took great pleasure in the spin move that put the other man's face up against the wall. "Don't even think about it, Burdick. Nobody," he gave Dustin's collar a slightly tightened shake to make his point stronger, "plays around with the value of a child like that, not in my presence. Got it?"

Dustin hadn't spent the last eight years staying in top form.

Matt had.

Whatever Dustin had been doing for money didn't pump up his triceps and biceps. His abs.

Building houses, hauling lumber, lifting windows and cabinets into place kept Matt on an Olympic-training regimen weekly. The reality of that knowledge shone in Dustin's nervous expression. He gave a quick nod, definitely in his best interest.

Good.

"And you'll sign the papers when you get them, and give them back to the courier who will then deliver them back here to Callie. Right?" He tightened Dustin's collar a smidge more, hoping he made his point.

Dustin nodded again. "Yes."

"Excellent." Matt loosened his hold but didn't back

off. "I love that kid. And I love his mother. And I didn't spend eight years in the marines *pretending* to be a man, so when those papers come, you open the envelope, sign where noted and send them back. Got it?"

"I said yes."

Matt angled his head slightly as Dustin faced him. "I heard you. I'm just making sure we understand each other."

Dustin blew out a breath. "If it gets me out of any more of her stupid court filings, we're good."

Matt had to take another step back. And nail his hands to his sides. And haul in a big breath. It had been a long time since the urge to pummel someone loomed with such ripe potential, but he pushed to keep his eye on the goal: making Jake his own. If Dustin signed off, Matt would be free to adopt Jake, if Callie gave her blessing.

Matt went back inside as Dustin strode off. He sat down, waiting for Don, his gut twisting. He couldn't make sense of walking out on a kid, maybe because it had happened to him. He'd lived the experience and suffered the fallout.

Why would God let that happen? Who watched out for little ones these days? Kids nudged aside by adult drama?

The strong words from the book of Joshua came back to him. "...then choose for yourselves this day who you shall serve...as for me and my house? We will serve the Lord."

That's what he wanted with Callie. The piece that

had been missing from his growing years. Not just a home. Or a family. He longed for a family of faith, hope and love. God-abiding. Together. A tiny light flickered within as Matt realized how Dustin had used Callie for his own amusement. He'd never intended to stay, to be the husband Callie deserved and the father Jake needed.

Matt had every intention of doing just that.

And as Don turned the corner from the corridor leading to the treatment rooms, Matt comprehended something else. Life had sideswiped Don, just as it had him. Sure, Don was the adult. He should have and could have reacted better. Maybe with faith, he would have, but Don had been taken out at the knees when he learned he was living a lie, that his wife had cheated on him and passed off someone else's child as his.

He came toward Matt, his face tired. Worn. Matt moved down the hall and braced him with a soldier's arm.

"I'm okay." Don tried to shrug him off, but Matt held tight.

"Hey, can't a kid help his old man now and again?"

Don's feet shuffled to a stop. He turned. Met Matt's gaze. "I—"

"Do you need a wheelchair to the car?"

Don shook his head. "No. Just a little tired."

"Then lean on me, Dad. It's not that far."

Don looked up at him. His light-eyed gaze grew moist. Matt had to choke back a lump in his own throat, a knot of regret for so much time wasted.

But that was over. He braced the older man and started forward. "I know where there's a pot of stew waiting. Should be just about done. And some fresh, homemade biscuits."

"It sounds good," Don admitted.

"Then let's go. You need to make another appointment?"

Don shook his head. "Not for a while."

"Good, because we got a boatload of plasterboard delivered today, and you need to rest up. We're going to have one busy winter."

Don's shoulders straightened. His chin came up. His step seemed just a little bit stronger. More invigorated. He gave a quick swipe to his eyes and nodded back at Matt. "I'm looking forward to it, son."

An old smile crept up on Matt, the kind of smile he used to share with his father, back in the day. He squeezed Don's arm as he led the way to the snow-filled parking lot, pretty sure his personal life paths had been freshly plowed, and glad of it. "Me, too."

Chapter Seventeen

"What's this?" Matt studied the envelope he received the next afternoon and quizzed the courier standing on the doorstep of the Cape Cod model. "Is this a summons?"

"I need your signature, sir."

Foreboding made Matt hesitate, then he clenched his jaw, signed the form and waited as the courier separated a copy for Matt's records.

He stepped into the quiet and nearly complete home, tore open the envelope and pulled out a sheaf of legal-looking documents. He scanned the information, got the gist of the contents, then sat down hard on the second step to read more carefully.

"…because the rules of due process were not followed in Mr. Marek's case, and because his ownership rights may have been revoked without due cause and/or proper documentation, Wellingtown General Bank will pay you a sum as decided by the appraisal firm of Littinger and Littinger in Olean, New York, as reparation. Amount due will include but will not be limited to wages paid, materials secured and monies invested to buy the afore-named subdivision 'Cobbled Creek.'

"Wellington General regrets any and all difficulties this transaction may cause and sincerely extends its apologies while accepting no blame for the mistaken foreclosure involved."

Mistaken foreclosure?

Reparation?

Had he just lost Cobbled Creek?

Matt stared at the paper and swallowed hard.

They were taking Cobbled Creek away from him. Could they do that?

"No," said his lawyer firmly a few minutes later when Matt got through to him on the newly installed landline. "They can't just send you a letter that says 'Oops, we goofed, sorry. Let's have a do-over.' This is their first step in trying to rectify a big mistake. They're hoping you'll give in gracefully so they don't look bad or careless, which is exactly what they were in this case and many others, using people to robo-sign documents."

"Robo-sign?"

The lawyer sighed. "Instead of having bank professionals read each document the way they're supposed to, some banks hired new graduates to handle the influx of foreclosure documentation the past couple of years. Their job was to count the pages, make sure they were all there, then sign off as the bank's representative."

"You're kidding."

"I wish I was. And none of this was obvious last

month when we closed. Then the scandal broke and banks started scrambling to put their houses in order."

"So I don't lose Cobbled Creek? Is that what you're saying?"

"We have to fight it, but yes, you will be able to keep the subdivision because it's their fault. Not yours. And then it's up to them to pay Hank Marek some sort of compensation for taking it over illegally. And making restitution for his loss of income."

"And his daughter's loss of income for those two years? Do they cover that?"

"No, that would be an indirect consequence unless she's listed as co-owner, but that wasn't the case."

How could he grasp this? Make sense of it? Half an hour ago he had his life mapped out before him, and it looked good. Sweet. Inviting.

Now?

One piece of mail and a bank's overeagerness to seize property put it all in jeopardy. "I need time to think, Jon. To figure this all out."

"There's no hurry," Jon told him, "but Hank Marek has most likely been notified at the same time you were. Just so you're prepared. He may pay you a visit."

"I'm living with him."

"You're what?"

It sounded weird considering this turn of events. "They let me stay in an extra room in their home because it adjoins the subdivision. And they've been working for me from the beginning."

"That's not a good situation to be in right now," the lawyer explained in a no-nonsense voice. "It's a conflict of interest at best and being professionally involved with a family you may bring litigation against could color your judgment."

"I thought it would be against the bank." Matt gripped the phone tighter. "You mean I might have to sue Hank?"

"Depending on how this plays out, yes. It's a numbers game, Matt. And a power play. But we've got the power because we have ownership."

"Illegally."

"Not on our end," the lawyer said roundly. "We had no information that led us to believe any of this had occurred. This is the bank's error. Not ours. They're just hoping you bow out gracefully."

Bow out gracefully? How about run screaming? "I've got to go, Jon. Think this through. Pray."

"Don't think too long. Wellington General is no slouch in the money department, and they'll cough up a nice piece of change, but we need to respond quickly."

A nice piece of change.

Is that what his hopes and dreams came down to? His attempt to come back home and make amends? Was he here to gain a "nice piece of change" at Hank's expense? At Callie's expense?

Callie.

His gut clenched as realization hit.

What would people think if he courted Callie now? If Hank regained ownership of Cobbled Creek? They would assume he was looking out for number one. People would see it as a ploy to maintain a Cavanaugh Construction interest in a lucrative business venture.

What should he do? What could he do? Sue the bank? That meant suing Hank's interest in Cobbled Creek as well.

What would Grandpa Gus do?

He'd pray, Matt realized. He'd pray hard, then man up and do the right thing, an upright man in all regards.

Matt climbed into his truck and drove north, away from the dream that just evaporated around him, knowing if he fought Hank on this, the entire lower half of the county would see what they'd come to believe twenty years before. A guy who put himself first, all the time.

He found a small church open in the college town of Houghton. He crept in the back door and found a quiet corner, a place to talk to God. Examine his options. And by the time he stood to leave a long while later, he knew exactly what he had to do, but didn't pretend acceptance. He'd be giving up his dream of a home with Callie. Of adopting Jake. Of being the father he'd never had, an upright man in all regards.

Keeping Cobbled Creek when Hank had been grievously wronged could never be considered right.

And the swirl of malicious gossip that would circle around Callie and Jake if he stayed in the picture was the very world he'd come back to fix. Not reinstigate. He wasn't a gold digger. Or a user. But marrying

Callie would look that way, and Matt knew firsthand how tongues would wag, mostly because he was involved and he hadn't been in town long enough to prove his worth.

Lousy timing, all told, not unlike what happened to Hank Marek a few years before.

He headed back toward Jamison and the life he thought he'd have, now gone, and couldn't act as if the journey didn't break his heart.

"You worked late, Dad," Callie observed as her father pushed through the side door that evening. "I'll start the burgers when Matt pulls in," she added, then nodded Jake's way. "And this guy's teacher says he's doing great, he's hardworking and focused and she's pleased with his progress. So we'll celebrate that with cupcakes later." She pulled a broiler pan from the lower cupboard, then turned toward her father more fully. His expression said something had gone wrong. Very wrong. "What's happened?"

Face set, Hank settled into a chair.

"Are you okay?"

He scowled and thumped the table with his fist. "Matt's gone."

"Matt's…" Callie worked her brain around her father's appearance, his accelerated breathing, his heightened color and…

Nope. Couldn't do it. She sat next to him and was surprised to see a sheen of moisture in his eyes. Army men didn't cry. Ever. "Dad, you're scaring me." She leaned closer, keeping her voice low. "What do you mean 'Matt's gone'?"

"He left. This afternoon. Packed up his stuff, signed Cobbled Creek back over to me and took off."

None of this was making any sense. "He signed Cobbled Creek over to you? What does that mean?"

Her father withdrew a bundle of papers from inside his jacket. "The bank messed up. They seized Cobbled Creek illegally. And now they want to fix things, which means they'll pay Matt to give it up."

"Illegally? How?"

"Not following procedures. So they notified Matt and me today and Matt got it in his head that he'd be better off bowing out and letting me take it back."

"But—"

"I know." Hank lifted his gaze to Callie's. "He *belongs* here. I felt it. You felt it. For pity's sake, *he* felt it, but then this." Hank grabbed the papers and lofted them into the air. "This happens and everything gets messed up."

"He left."

"Yes."

Without saying goodbye. Because that was the story of her life, it shouldn't come as any big surprise.

Callie stood, her legs wooden, her jaw tight. Suddenly the act of flipping burgers seemed like too much work.

But there was Jake to think of. What would he think when he found out Matt had left? How would he react?

She moved back to the kitchen, her head spinning, trying to make sense of things and failing, but she knew one thing. She'd stepped out of her comfort zone and trusted a man whose heart seemed to match hers. Kind. Caring. Loving to build, to see beautiful things rise from the ground, take shape against a God-given sky.

She'd been stupid. Again.

Old doubts consumed her. How needy was she that Matt's bright smile and sweet compliments won her over so quickly? Hadn't she wondered from the beginning?

Yes.

But she'd let foolish hopes and dreams color her judgment, pull her off task. Make her think Matt really cared about her. About Jake.

Jake.

He'd be brokenhearted, and it was all her fault.

Regret warred with anger and sadness, a sorry threesome. Simple math filled in the rest. Matt would get bank money for Cobbled Creek and her father would have his business back. For a win-win situation, this felt like a total loss.

She swallowed tears around a lump the size of a stair runner and slapped ground beef together with way more power than necessary, but better to take her anger out on meat than on her father. Or her son. Or…

No, that's right, Matt wouldn't be around anymore. At all. Ever. And just like that her hopes and dreams disappeared in the blink of an eye. Just as well, really. Better to count on herself. She knew that. And she'd be fine. Just fine.

"Can we play Christmas music, Mom?" Jake poked his head up from an internet site about the battle at Midway. "And did Grandpa forget to turn on the Christmas lights?"

"I did." Hank pushed to his feet, looking anything but festive. "I'll see to it right now."

"When's Matt coming?" Jake continued. "I'm starved."

Callie ignored the first question by zeroing in on the second. "I'll make the burgers. They can always be warmed up later."

"Okay."

She wanted to shout that Matt wasn't coming back. That he'd moved out. Moved on. He had his money and he'd taken the quickest path north. But she couldn't say any of that, couldn't even think it without wanting to bawl her eyes out. Except soldiers don't do that. They keep on, keepin' on.

By the time Jake went to bed, Callie felt numb. Numb from pretending, numb from fielding questions, from avoiding the looks of concern her father shot her.

Mind-bending numb, but nothing an all-night crying jag wouldn't cure. And she was headed that way when her father stopped her. "So, what are you going to do?"

"Do?" She raised her shoulders, dropped them and shook her head. "About?"

"Matt."

"Matt's gone, Dad. End of story."

Hank stared at her, then swiped a hand across his face. "You're not getting this, are you?"

"That Matt needs distance, he's got his money and he booked out of here like a race car driver? I'm getting it just fine, Dad."

"No." Hank settled his hands on her shoulders and met her anger with compassion. "He didn't leave because he didn't want to be with you. With us."

"Um, right." Callie sent him a look of disbelief and when he smiled, she had to remember why it was wrong to fight with your father.

"He left because he thinks it's the *right* thing to do."

"That makes no sense."

"It makes perfect sense," Hank countered. "Matt came here and helped our dream come true, but when that letter came today he realized we'd been wronged. That the bank acted too quickly. And that wasn't fair."

"So he left without saying goodbye to me or Jake? Right. Thanks for the pep talk, Dad."

She moved to step away, but Hank wouldn't let her. "He loves you."

Callie snorted. Very unfeminine, but then that was the story of her life. Unloved. Unfeminine. Uncherished.

"He does," her father insisted, "but think about this from his perspective. Either he loses Cobbled Creek or he fights us for it. Matt cares for us and doesn't want to hurt us."

"Very altruistic of him. But he still fled for places unknown without saying goodbye, therefore final chapter. End of story."

"It's nothing of the sort, and you've got your mother's stubbornness," Hank replied. "How will it look to people if Matt starts showing interest in you after he's had to relinquish the subdivision?"

"I—"

"Like he's a gold digger. Like he's trying to hang on. People talk, Callie."

"I don't care what people say," she told him, but a sheen of reality started to seep through. "Why would Matt?"

"Because Matt was talked about for years," her father reminded her. "And he came back here to fix things, not stir them up. He'd never want you and Jake to be targeted by gossip."

"You mean…"

"People might think he was after you to maintain his interest in Cobbled Creek."

"But that's ridiculous."

Hank's arched brow said it wasn't ridiculous. It was quite possible, actually, the way some small-town tongues wagged. "You're sure, Dad? Because I'm not a big risk-taker anymore."

Hank leaned closer. "I'm one-hundred-percent sure. I asked Maude to make a blanket for you a bunch of years back. A quilt that reminded me of your mother. All flowery and pretty, like spring."

Callie nodded, unsure where this was going.

"Then things went bad and I couldn't pay for the

blanket. Maude hung on to it, and I went into town the other day to buy it."

"What's this got to do with—"

"It was gone," Hank continued as if she hadn't spoken. "Matt bought it for you. Maude said she wrapped it up real pretty. Said she knew he was smitten weeks ago and told him about the quilt, and he told her he was going to make sure Callie had the best Christmas ever."

Tears pricked her eyes, but they were different tears. Tears of anticipation and hope, not anger. "He bought it for me?"

"Yes, but probably has no clue how to fix this whole mess because of a stupid bank mistake. Do you love him?" Hank's direct question put it all on the line.

"Yes." Callie met her father's gaze. "Oh, yes."

"Then show him."

Callie's mind spun with this new assortment of facts, but she recognized one thing: Her father was right. If this was going to get fixed, Callie needed to be the one to do it because while Matt might be handy with tools, he was a proud marine, first and last. And a marine would never shackle those he loved with rumor and speculation. It was up to her to show him the way to the family he never had. If the guy wasn't too proud and stubborn to see what God had laid before him, that is. "I will, Dad, but I'll need your help. Can you call him? Get him to come back here tomorrow evening? And meet you at the model home?"

Hank grinned. "Will do. And Callie?"

She turned from the stairs and met his gaze.

"I'm proud of you, honey."

And she felt it, right to her toes. She met his smile and returned it. "Thank you, Dad."

Chapter Eighteen

Matt saw Hank's caller I.D. and hated to answer the phone, but he did. "Hello."

"Matt?"

"Yes, Hank. What's up?"

A slight pause tempted Matt to ask about Callie. About Jake. How things were going. It had been one whole day, after all.

Pathetic, Cavanaugh.

"Can you meet me at the model house later today?"

The house Callie loved? "How about we meet in town instead? I'm staying at my brother's place in Wellsville while we get things resituated."

"I'm tied up all day." Apology laced Hank's tone. "And I need to go over a few things with you about the model and the house that's sold. I'd do it here, but…"

Matt understood. Callie would be there. So would Jake. And he wasn't in any shape to see them right now, to witness his sacrifice firsthand.

You don't have to give up anything, son.

Grandpa Gus's wisdom poked him from within.

God's offered you a wonderful chance, the chance to love. Grab it. Run with it. Embrace it.

Right. And have the whole town think he was scrambling to hang on to Cobbled Creek through Callie? Honor first, and that meant Callie first, in this instance. Subjecting Jake and Callie to the gossip mill he'd lived with all his life? Wasn't gonna happen. Not on his watch.

Pride and dismay clenched his gut as he angled the truck down Cobbled Creek Lane that evening. He didn't look toward the Marek house to see their tree winking softly in the side window, or the string of lights he'd helped Callie hang in the rain. Or Shadow Jesus.

The memory of Jake's upturned face C-clamped Matt's heart, his earnest explanations about Bethlehem. Mary and Joseph and a child born to the poor. The little guy paid such close attention to detail, a rare trait, Matt thought; but then, Jake was no ordinary child. He was Callie's son.

The clamp tightened its screw hold on Matt's heart as he approached the model home, the pretty walkway welcoming him.

Should he ring the bell? Walk in?

Swallowing frustration, he pushed open the door and called Hank's name.

"Dad's not here."

Callie.

His heart jumped, then sank. "He was supposed to meet me."

She came forward, looking absolutely wonderful, but then he felt that way when she donned triple layers and flannels to work side by side with him. But tonight the one-shoulder top over fitted jeans left no doubt that Callie Marek was in good shape.

And breathtakingly beautiful.

Matt scrubbed a hand to his neck and looked around. Her presence made his determination to stay away seem somewhat dumb. And maybe impossible. But he was doing it for her, he reminded himself as she drew closer.

"You left."

He nodded, holding himself arm's length away when what he longed to do was reach out and touch her. Slide that curl tickling her cheek back behind her ear.

"It seemed best."

"For whom?"

He waved a hand. "Everyone."

She encroached a little more. "Really?"

"Yes." He thought so at the time anyway, but right now, with Callie so near, smelling Christmas-cookie sweet, he wasn't so sure. Which meant he should take a step back. He did.

Callie followed.

"Cal, listen…"

"No, you listen, marine." She closed the distance between them and gave him a very unromantic thwack on the arm. "What on earth are you doing, Matt Cavanaugh?"

"Trying to find your father and settle our affairs."

She sighed out loud. "Not with him. With me." She

waved a hand between them. "Us. Because here's how I see things, and let me just add, it's pretty obvious that you and my father need a woman around and you should be thanking God I'm available."

Available as in…

"First of all—" he didn't think it was possible for her to move closer, and yet she did, wagging her pointer finger in the air "—you love me."

Honor, integrity and honesty disallowed a lie. "Yes."

Callie rolled her eyes. "You could try to sound a little happier about it."

"Callie—"

"Ah." She put two sweet-smelling fingers to his mouth to shush him, the feel and scent reminding him of those shared kisses. The hopes and dreams he'd thought possible the past weeks. "Still my turn. And you love Jake."

"Who couldn't?"

She smiled up at him, and he realized she wasn't wearing heels. She was, in fact, just wearing socks, looking way too cozy and at home, but then, this house fit her as if…

"Here's my proposal," she went on as if sealing a business deal. "You get all this nonsense about what people will think, about giving up your dream and handing over Cobbled Creek to my dad out of your head."

"But—"

"In lieu of that we form a partnership of sorts."

Her slanted smile released the clamp on Matt's heart a bit more. "Are you suggesting a merger?"

Her smile deepened. She poked him in the chest. "Exactly that." She couldn't get any closer without touching him, so she did, letting her hair riffle against his chin, his neck. Then she squared her shoulders. "Of course there are terms to negotiate."

"I'm a great negotiator."

"I don't doubt it for a minute," she agreed amicably, as if they weren't discussing very serious things like weddings. Babies.

Unless he misunderstood her.

One look into those pretty green eyes nixed that. "You know I was no choirboy, Cal." Despite the lure, the attraction, the love, he didn't want Callie blindsided ever again. About anything. "My past might trip us up from time to time."

She met his gaze straight on. "It could, but I'm going to trust God to get us through whatever happens. Once I get it through that thick head of yours that it's okay to love us." She reached up and feathered a soft kiss to his jaw.

"Stop." He put up a hand and stepped back. Confusion swam in her eyes until he dropped to one knee and grasped her hand. "If we're going to do this, we're going to do it right."

Her mouth formed a perfect O, and then she smiled, delighted. "Please do."

He squeezed her fingers and held her gaze, wishing she could see his heart. His soul. "Callie, you are the most incredible and beautiful woman I've ever known. You have a heart of gold and you're really good with power tools."

A bubble of laughter mixed with the sheen of tears in her eyes.

"Will you marry me? Share your life and son with me? Grow old with me, building houses?"

"Homes," she corrected, and drew him up. "Not houses, Matt. Homes. And yes, I'll marry you. Have your babies. And work beside you all my days."

Matt lost himself in the feel of Callie's arms, her kiss, her presence, feeling like he'd come back to a home he'd never really had.

Lights burst on around them. Twinkle lights. They lined the windows of the first floor, and a tree, a real Christmas tree, lit up the soft yellow great room at the back of the house. Matt hugged Callie and grinned as Hank and the guys tried unsuccessfully to slip quietly out the back.

"Jake."

The boy broke ranks with the older men and raced back into the house. He barreled into Callie and Matt and Matt tipped the boy's chin up to hold his gaze. "Jake, I'd like your permission to marry your mother. I love her and I love you and I think we'd make a great family together. What do you think?"

Jake's face beamed as bright as the Bethlehem star, a symbol of a new beginning. A new hope. "I say yes."

"And," Matt shifted his gaze to the pretty woman in his left arm, a woman who'd known pain and abandonment but was wise enough to let God guide her through it all, step by step, "I think we should live here."

"Here?" Callie swept the model with the wistful look she'd tried to contain weeks before.

"Right here. If we're going to forge a family business, we need proximity. Affordability. And," he let his eyes twinkle into hers, "it's a four bedroom which means growth potential."

Callie blushed.

Jake laughed and fist pumped the air. "And I get to help you and Grandpa build, Matt!"

Matt ruffled a hand through Jake's hair and dropped another kiss to Callie's smiling mouth, wondering how he'd ever considered walking away. "You sure do, son. You sure do."

Epilogue

"Oh, look." Callie pointed to the left of the auditorium stage the following December and gave a mom-like wave. "There's Jake. Right next to Jordan."

Chloe Wiseman leaned across her husband. "They're peas in a pod, those two. Have I mentioned often enough how happy we are to live in Cobbled Creek? Near you guys? To have such a nice friend for Jordan, so close?"

Callie laughed and squeezed the other woman's hand. "I feel the same way. And we've got a great bunch of neighbors with Phase One complete."

A tiny noise erupted from Callie's left. "Dad, you okay over there?"

Hank rearranged the pink-swaddled bundle in his arms and gave a sage nod. "Nothing a bottle and a burp won't cure. But I'm still not loving the pink camo."

"It's adorable," Callie protested.

"It's pink," Hank argued. "Camo should never be pink."

"Well, she is a girl," Matt reminded him. He

shrugged and met Hank's grin. "Pink goes with the territory. Doesn't it, Morgan?" Matt leaned in and ran a finger along the tiny girl's soft-as-down cheek.

"Dresses, fine." Hank kept his voice army-gruff, but his eyes twinkled as the newborn accepted the bottle with fisted hands and greedy tugs. "But army gear should be army gear. Never the twain shall meet."

Matt leaned closer to Callie. "What's he going to think of the pink leopard print stuff Hannah gave us?"

Callie laughed, Hank made a face and Matt watched with pride as Jake *Cavanaugh* stepped up to the microphone to welcome people to the eighteenth annual Christmas Concert for Veterans. And when Jake found them in the crowd and sent a grin their way, Matt felt like Grandpa Gus just clapped him on the back, showing his full approval.

And it felt good.

* * * * *

Dear Reader,

I love stories that laud success over failure, new beginnings and second chances! As a child of two alcoholic parents, I understand Matt Cavanaugh's childhood, but by the grace of God I attended a Catholic school filled with dedicated Christian staff. Their warmth, understanding and diligence taught me to move above and beyond. To grasp faith and hope when darkness surrounded me.

Callie Marek is a gal who can put her hand to any task, like my mother-in-law. I forged Callie's character to reflect Mom's strength and stoicism. Callie's mistake was falling for a man who didn't realize her worth, a woman unafraid to get dirty, dig out a pond or run power tools. Women like this helped build our country and I was determined that Hank's wonderful daughter would find a match worthy of her in God's good time.

And she did, she just had to slap some sense into our proud marine toward the end! A marine who determined the right course for life and stuck to it, doggedly, despite his early mistakes. Thank you for reading *Yuletide Hearts,* my first Christmas story for Love Inspired! Feel free to visit me at menofalleganycounty.com, or stop by Ruthy's Place at ruthysplace.com or check out things at www.ruthloganherne.com. We've got a constant party going on at www.seekerville.blogspot.com where you'll find a strong Christian sisterhood sharing advice and cyber food! You can also snail-mail me c/o Love Inspired Books, 233 Broadway Suite 1001, New York, NY 10279. I love hearing from you!

Ruth Logan Herne

Questions for Discussion

1. This book opens as Matt Cavanaugh questions himself about buying Cobbled Creek. Have you ever taken a leap of faith and doubted yourself? How did that come out in the end?

2. Jake and The General exemplify all that is right and simple in the world of Christmas. What are the simple things in your world that you tend to overlook or forget to thank God for?

3. Callie comes face-to-face with her father's gut-wrenching financial ruin when she realizes that Matt has taken over the subdivision. At this time she doesn't realize how nicely God has answered her prayer. Have you ever experienced a time when your prayers are answered unbeknown to you until later?

4. Matt has to swallow his pride and ask the Mareks to work for him. Do you have a hard time asking others for help? Or making amends with those you've hurt, even unintentionally?

5. Callie agrees to work for Matt because money is tight. In saying yes, Callie opens herself up to possibilities she can't take. Matt is her boss and a bad romance could ruin this opportunity.

Has God ever put mixed opportunities in front of you? How did they work out?

6. Callie cannot trust her heart. She married her ex-husband while stationed in Iraq, serving her country. But he abandoned her and their baby, leaving them without money or care. Callie guards her heart beneath a tough armor. Have you ever had to take a leap of faith? To trust God to catch you if you fall?

7. Shadow Jesus is Jake's favorite Christmas decoration. The silhouetted figures are simple and holy against the faded house at night. The humble nativity opens Matt's heart and reminds him of Christ's difficult beginnings. Does remembering the true nativity story help you keep the heart in Christmas?

8. Matt realizes he must mend his relationship with Don Cavanaugh, but it's hard to forgive him. Don's illness and earnest quest to stay sober soften Matt's heart toward forgiveness. Did Don's efforts help ease the way to a new relationship?

9. Callie's self-image suffered with Dustin's treatment of her. She's a survivor, but her womanly ego was injured. Matt's respect for her ability and her efforts offer her hope. Why is it so important for us to gain others' approval? Is that healthy?

10. Matt's got a lot on his plate, but he's come back to town to make amends. Once he begins with Don, he finds everything else easier. Do you find it hard to make that first step toward reconciliation or commitment, but once made, the path gets easier? Why is that?

11. God has blessed Callie with a beautiful son, but Jake's father cares nothing for the boy or his mother. How difficult is it to explain a parent's indifference to a child and what kind of effect might that have on Jake?

12. Matt longs to make a family with Callie and Jake, but his world gets turned upside down when he realizes that Hank and Callie lost their business illegally. An honorable man, he feels he has to walk away. If Callie hadn't intervened, would Matt have come back on his own, or would he see that door as closed forevermore?

13. Meeting Matt at the model home is a big step forward for Callie. How did Matt's confidence in her abilities and his appreciation for her beauty help build her self-esteem and bring them to their happy ending?

LARGER-PRINT BOOKS!

**GET 2 FREE
LARGER-PRINT NOVELS
PLUS 2 FREE
MYSTERY GIFTS**

Larger-print novels are now available...

YES! Please send me 2 FREE LARGER-PRINT Love Inspired® novels and my 2 FREE mystery gifts (gifts are worth about $10). After receiving them, if I don't wish to receive any more books, I can return the shipping statement marked "cancel". If I don't cancel, I will receive 6 brand-new novels every month and be billed just $4.99 per book in the U.S. or $5.49 per book in Canada. That's a saving of at least 23% off the cover price. It's quite a bargain! Shipping and handling is just 50¢ per book in the U.S. and 75¢ per book in Canada.* I understand that accepting the 2 free books and gifts places me under no obligation to buy anything. I can always return a shipment and cancel at any time. Even if I never buy another book, the two free books and gifts are mine to keep forever.

122/322 IDN FEG3

Name _____ (PLEASE PRINT)

Address _____ Apt. #

City _____ State/Prov. _____ Zip/Postal Code

Signature (if under 18, a parent or guardian must sign)

Mail to the **Reader Service:**
IN U.S.A.: P.O. Box 1867, Buffalo, NY 14240-1867
IN CANADA: P.O. Box 609, Fort Erie, Ontario L2A 5X3

Not valid to current subscribers to Love Inspired Larger-Print books.

**Are you a current subscriber to Love Inspired books
and want to receive the larger-print edition?
Call 1-800-873-8635 or visit www.ReaderService.com.**

* Terms and prices subject to change without notice. Prices do not include applicable taxes. Sales tax applicable in N.Y. Canadian residents will be charged applicable taxes. Offer not valid in Quebec. This offer is limited to one order per household. All orders subject to credit approval. Credit or debit balances in a customer's account(s) may be offset by any other outstanding balance owed by or to the customer. Please allow 4 to 6 weeks for delivery. Offer available while quantities last.

Your Privacy—The Reader Service is committed to protecting your privacy. Our Privacy Policy is available online at www.ReaderService.com or upon request from the Reader Service.

We make a portion of our mailing list available to reputable third parties that offer products we believe may interest you. If you prefer that we not exchange your name with third parties, or if you wish to clarify or modify your communication preferences, please visit us at www.ReaderService.com/consumerschoice or write to us at Reader Service Preference Service, P.O. Box 9062, Buffalo, NY 14269. Include your complete name and address.

LILP11B

Love Inspired® SUSPENSE
RIVETING INSPIRATIONAL ROMANCE

Watch for our series of edge-
of-your-seat suspense novels.
These contemporary tales
of intrigue and romance
feature Christian characters
facing challenges to their faith...
and their lives!

AVAILABLE IN REGULAR & LARGER-PRINT FORMATS

For exciting stories that reflect traditional values,
visit:
www.ReaderService.com